Nano-Novellas of New York

An Anthology of Short Stories about New
York City People, Places and Things

By Paul Conley

ISBN 978-0-578-00620-8

A Wish For Angela and Jillian

The true measure of a person is not that they are perfect
Perfect people never have to overcome adversity
Perfect people never have to fix their mistakes
Perfect people never have to stress
Perfect people never have to work hard
In summary, perfect people are boring

I don't want you to be perfect
I want you to be who you are
I want to work with you to get where you want to go
I want to share with you all I know
So you can learn from my mistakes as well as your own.

The journey is as important as the result.
I want to work hard to become a better human being
I want to work hard to make my tiny corner of the world a little better after I
leave.

You are not perfect. Neither am I.
I am okay with that, as long as we help each other out.
I am okay with that as long as we both do our best.
In all that we do.
And help each other
And learn from each other
And love each other

Contents

The Promise of December 29th

The Promise of December 29th is set in Grand Central Terminal and is a story of the enduring friendship of four very disparate men who share a love for singing and 1950's style doo-wop.

The Promise of December 29th

Grand Central Terminal is located in the heart of Midtown Manhattan

and is the largest train station in the world. But Grand Central is much

more than just an ordinary, functional, run of the mill train station. It is

a dazzling microcosm of the city it inhabits. Like Manhattan, much of it

is opulent, grandiose and somewhat ostentatious. Its main concourse is

longer than a football field with a ceiling over 150 feet high. Huge

windows reach for the ceiling in the shape of arches, while spiral

staircases amble elegantly upward to the mezzanine. Its ceiling was

painted by the French artist Paul Helleu in a zodiac pattern based on a

medieval manuscript.   If you didn't know it was a train terminal, you

might mistake the main concourse for a museum or an opera house.

Yet, a visitor to Grand Central is also presented with disparity and incongruity. Grand Central is majestic and regal one moment, and gritty and coarse the next. Fast food kiosks reside next to fine restaurants and shops. Captains of industry walk side by side with vagrants and common criminals. And despite the opulent surroundings, customary manners are in short supply as people rush by, bunched in crowded clusters, bouncing off each other like pin balls.

Only tourists seem to linger to enjoy the beauty of this landmark. Commuters are intent on racing to get to their jobs or appointments, oblivious to their unique surroundings. Over 750,000 people pass through Grand Central every day; most of them, it seems, are in such an intense rush to get somewhere else you would think there was nothing special about this place. Yet there actually is something special; something almost magical about this place. All you have to do is slow down a little and keep your eyes and ears open. If you do, you will find it.

Tony had arrived at Grand Central about 4:30 this afternoon. He stood alone leaning against the wall in a hallway off the Main Concourse. He was the first of his group to arrive. He waited in the cramped passage leading into the subway, away from the spacious, high ceilings and opulence of the grand hall. He preferred it here. The ceiling was low and the hallway was narrow. He could hear everything so vividly. He was close to the people as they whizzed by, so he could almost feel what they were thinking. They were strangers, but he somehow knew what was inside of them. Some were stressed, some were happy, some were angry. What was great about this place was that everyone was feeling something. Tony thought the worst thing in the world would be to feel nothing. He always thought that hell is not to feel bad all the time; but to feel nothing all the time.

People rushed by, paying him no mind. And he was fine with that. He liked living anonymously, blending in with the multitude, just living his life. He was the proverbial every man; he lived a good life in his small house on a side street in Queens and he was happy. His job as a postman had allowed him to meet people, greet people and be outside walking every day all these years. He looked fit for a grandfather of 63 and was a good father and a good husband for over 35 years. He could always be found at 5:30 at the dinner table with his wife Donna. But he would miss dinner tonight. It was December 29th and dinner had to wait. He looked up at the big gray letter S on the wall. This was where they would meet again at 5:00, under the sign for the Times Square Shuttle, just like every December 29th since 1963. He waited patiently.

Meanwhile, in a large penthouse office in Midtown Manhattan, high above Park Avenue, Jerry looked out at the City below. He had risen to the head post at Simkus Lawrey, the third largest private equity firm in the world. His firm bought and sold companies and made a lot of money doing it. It was hard work and he was good at it. He had probably read a million financial statements in his life. He was incisive, industrious and diligent. He loved looking and searching for that clue that would lead him to find value, where others thought there was none.

Jerry usually worked late, until 10:00 most nights, but he loved it. Each transaction was different and exciting. Doing all the deals was invigorating. He liked taking risk and he got a sense of satisfaction from competing in such a spirited arena. It reminded him of his days playing basketball at Princeton. His senior year, his team had advanced all the way to the finals of the Eastern Regional of the NCAA tournament. He was proud that he had been a part of that.

His office walls were paneled in wood and the room was filled with large mahogany furniture. It was strategically furnished to impress any visitors that ventured in. Mementos from his storied career were scattered throughout: his picture with Pete Carrill and Bill Bradley, his picture of his fishing trip with the President, the tombstone for his takeover of ABC Industries. His office also contained several precious paintings and sculptures of the artist Frederic Remington. Remington's western themes of cowboys, Indians, horses and wide open landscapes were lively and adventurous. They inspired Jerry to dream.

It's a funny thing about dreams, though. Sometimes dreams look great in your head, but they aren't quite as great when they actually happen. Jerry had always dreamed about being wealthy and powerful and was driven to pursue that dream. No one worked harder than Jerry and he was wealthier than he could have ever imagined as a kid growing up in Queens. But, although he loved his work, sometimes it seemed like he did it simply because he knew no other way. As Jerry gazed out his window, he was interrupted by a telephone call. His assistant reminded him of his annual meeting on December 29th at 5:00. Jerry put on his coat and rushed out the door. He took the elevator down to the street and briskly walked south towards Grand Central Terminal.

In Flushing, Tommy boarded the crowded Number Seven train. He had to get to Grand Central Terminal in Manhattan promptly at 5:00. He had just finished coaching a practice with his basketball team at Holy Cross High School. He had been coaching basketball for over 30 years and, at 63 years old, he was finding each year harder and harder to keep up with the kids. This year's team didn't have as much talent as some other years, but the kids were coming around and he was excited about getting them ready for their game with arch rival St. Francis Prep in a week and a half.

Tommy had spent all these years teaching and coaching. He saw it all; good kids, bad kids and every kind of kid in between. His dad had spent his whole adult life hating his job, dreading every new day. Tommy was glad he never hated his job like that. When Dad talked about "the depression", Tommy didn't know if Dad was referring to the country's time in the 1930's, when no one had a job, or his dad's very own life in the 1950's & 1960's when everyone had a job. In dad's case, a job he hated. Dad was always so unhappy; always worrying, always afraid, always complaining. I hate complaining, Tommy thought.

Usually Tommy didn't like riding the crowded trains; he preferred driving his SUV. Even if there was traffic, he could listen to the radio and get the news and sports report. But today is December 29th, and Tommy always takes the train on December 29th. As he looked around at the faces on the crowded train, most were tired or annoyed or in their own private worlds, reading newspapers, staring at blackberries and listening to I-Pods and cell phones. Tommy hummed an old song to himself as he looked around the train. He would soon be at Grand Central Terminal. He smiled.

In Lower Manhattan, Billy punched out from his job as a maintenance man at a building near Wall Street. It had been a long, hard twelve hour day because there were problems with the boiler. Still, he was happy to get some overtime pay this close to Christmas. That meant he could probably pay off the family's credit card bill, which was a rarity for the month of January. As Billy left the building and walked towards the subway, he silently cursed the boiler, though and wished it had decided to act up on any day other than today, December 29th. His hands were dirty and his uniform was greasy. He had wanted to wash up before his meeting at 5:00, but unfortunately there would be no time. He walked down the stairs and then ran to catch an Uptown train. He should be able to make it by 5:00, he thought.

As Billy boarded the subway car to Grand Central, he was surrounded by commuters with well-pressed suits and trendy wool coats. As Billy settled in, he encountered that look that he had seen before so many times. The gentleman next to him moved to another part of the train. This time he didn't know whether it was because he was filthy or because he was black. It didn't matter much either way; their eyes always said they weren't entirely comfortable with Old Billy. He used to get angry about it, but getting angry never helped him feel any better about it. The most painful time in his life was when he was a young militant; when he was the most resentful and angry about things. Hate swallowed his energy back then, as well as his happiness. Billy recalled that old saying of Franklin Roosevelt; the only thing to fear is fear itself. Billy thought he should have said this: the only thing to *hate* is *hate* itself.

Billy now thought that it was better to just accept what you couldn't change and only worry about what you could change, yourself. He couldn't change them and trying to change them would only frustrate him. They were the problem, not him. Billy knew he lived life the right way and that he had been blessed with a beautiful wife, two great kids and friends that would never break a promise to him, especially on December 29th. Looking at his watch, Billy could see he would not be late for his 5:00 appointment at Grand Central after all. He smiled broadly.

Back at Grand Central Terminal, Tony spied a tall distinguished man in a blue pinstriped suit and a camel hair overcoat in the distance. The man moved stylishly through the crowd. His white hair was combed straight back and his brown eyes sparkled as he approached. "Jerry!" Tony cried out, "You are usually the last one to get here."

Jerry replied, "I had to get here early this year. I am so sincerely happy to see you. I meet so many phony baloneys every day. I am getting tired of it. I want to lay it all out there this year. I really want to rock." Jerry gave Tony a bear hug, as the commuters rushed by.

As the two men chatted they were soon joined by two others. Jerry bellowed, "Look who's here Tony, it's Tommy and Billy. Right on time again. Gimme a hug, Billy."

"I didn't wash up, man. I ain't gonna get that fancy suit of yours dirty."

"Never mind the suit. I haven't seen you since last year," said Jerry as he hugged Billy tightly. Tony smiled widely as the two men separated. Tommy laughed out loud. The stylish camel hair overcoat was now smeared with a very unstylish oil stain. Immediately following Jerry's bear hug the eyes of all four men met. It was time.

The four men formed a tight circle, as the throngs of commuters raced by. A young police officer in the corner eyed them suspiciously.

These fellows don't belong together, he thought. They're all about the same age, but they don't look like they have anything in common. One guy looks like a millionaire, another looks like a bum, the other two look like regular Joes. Something strange is happening. He decided to approach.

But before the policeman could utter a word, the four men, Tony, Jerry, Tommy and Billy snapped their fingers in unison and broke out in song, "Oh oh yes I'm the Great Pretender, oo wa oo." The cop backed off. He had never heard more perfect harmony. Their voices were flawless. They knew all the words. The acoustics in this place, with its marble floors and stone walls, were phenomenal. The men spun together and danced magically in the small space in the hall as if their movements had been choreographed for years.

The police officer was spellbound. He now recalled his grandfather and the stories grandpa told him about singing with his friends on the stoop in the Bronx during the early 1960's. Music chimed from every corner. And no one needed microphones, instruments, light shows or amplifiers. It was all a cappella. Everything was pure; just the voices of four or five friends blending together like a miniature symphony.

A group of kids from Belmont Avenue even had a couple of number one hits, Grandpa said. Grandpa said those were magic times, the best times ever. Watching these four old guys, the police officer could now understand the meaning of what his grandfather spoke. This was friendship. This is doo wop. Now I get it!

A crowd gathered, mesmerized. The foot traffic in the corridor stopped and people watched the show. The performance had begun, just like it had every December 29th since 1963, when the four friends first performed as 18 year olds; when they promised each other that they would meet here on this day every year to perform, no matter what. Members of the crowd tossed money at their feet.

Tony urged the crowd, "Take your money back and give it to someone who really needs it. Maybe your pennies will cure cancer someday! We're here because we love doing this in this place. We just want to create some magic tonight. Bring it home and tell your kids about it."

And with that the four continued to sing and dance. Commuters stopped in their tracks, gaping at the show unfolding before them. Song after song echoed through the hall as the crowd swelled to several hundred. People stopped, putting away their cell phones, blackberries and I-Pods to simply listen. For a short time, this little piece of the world, which usually was in such a rush, slowed down. The words, melodies and harmonies of the past were revived again, this night, for all to enjoy. People were still stamping their feet, dancing, clapping and laughing as the show went into its third hour. Until finally the four closed the show, with a melodious rendition of the old Platters song, "Smoke Gets In Your Eyes."

As the crowd dispersed, the four friends congratulated themselves. This had been their best performance ever. "Same time next year?" asked Tommy.

"Absolutely" said Jerry.

"Definitely" said Billy.

"I hope so," said Tony with a little tear in the corner of his eye. "That was a damn good show. If it is our last one together, then we went out in style. But I gotta tell you guys something. I have cancer; they just found it, and it's inoperable. I start chemo tomorrow. I want you to get someone to replace me so you guys can keep doing this. I always thought Sam Cooke would have sounded good with us, but he isn't available. Unfortunately I guess I will be joining him soon."

The previously suspicious police officer, who was still on duty, overheard the group. He felt something inside himself, urging him to approach them. He quickly followed that impulse, walked towards the four men and said sheepishly, "I heard what you asked for and I would be honored to audition for your group."

Tommy looked at him and said, "I see by your badge that your name is Ray Wallace, son. We used to play ball against a Ray Wallace. He went to St. Raymond's in the Bronx. He was a great ballplayer. Really quick; a good ball handler. I heard he could sing a little too."

"That's my grandfather," said the police officer.

"Really; what's he doing now?" asked Tommy.

The officer spoke dejectedly, "He worked for years driving a local truck route. But cancer got him too. He died a couple of years ago. He would have loved to have seen your act tonight."

"Yeah we had a good time tonight, we rocked it," said Tommy. He paused, "So show us what you've got, kid."

And with that, the uniformed police officer sang. He didn't know how, but he miraculously knew the words to all the songs the group sang that night. He belted out two songs, "Why Do Fools Fall In Love" and "Teenager In Love". He sang the songs flawlessly and effortlessly, as if he had sung them many times before. Amazing, he thought. It was as if Grandpa actually was there with him, helping him along. When he finished, he asked, "Shall I join you here next year?"

Before anyone else could answer, Tony said, "Congratulations. If I'm here next year, you're our fifth. We'll sing five-part. If I'm not, you guys have a new fourth, the esteemed Mr. Ray Wallace. Now listen! I want you all here next year, December 29th at 5:00 P.M. sharp. Peace." And instantly the four friends bid each other farewell and went their separate ways.

The police officer was now alone. He gazed down the once crowded passage. It was silent and it was empty. He heard a voice in the distance softly whisper, "Good job, Ray."

Center

Center is a story of baseball and how a simple game can bond families and friends together.

Offensive players are required to "carry all gloves and other equipment off the field while their team is at bat." [Major League Baseball Rule 3.14. Amended in 1954]

Center

Memories are wondrous things. Sometimes they make you anxious; sometimes they make you happy; sometimes they make you sad; sometimes they make you laugh; sometimes they make you cry. They are not alive; but when you sit still and silent, alone with your thoughts, memories are often more real, more significant, than the events right in front of you. Memories are the roadmap to your soul. They tell you who you were, who you are and who you will be.

Today, one last time, I drive to my Aunt Teresa's house, the house where my late father grew up. Teresa is going to live in a nursing home from now on and she wants me to take things from the house; things she thinks will be sentimentally valuable to me. Although I am very busy with my own family, I feel obligated to go. After all, she was like my grandmother. She raised my father from the time he was twelve, when both their mother and father passed away. She was only twenty years old at the time, but she assumed dad's guardianship. Although a large responsibility for someone so young, it was her duty and she accepted it. Even at that young age, she had the character and resolve to take the right and honorable course; even if it was the more

difficult course. People of my generation aren't so selfless, it seems.

You rarely see such old world character, such courage, anymore.

I do not expect to find anything of great monetary value; there are no

robber barons in my genealogy. But I do expect to find a few valuable

treasures- some year books, perhaps some old pictures and trinkets, that

will give me a glimpse into their childhood and my heritage. As I drive

toward the house, my consciousness is filled with memories of my

childhood visits with Aunt Teresa and thoughts of my dad, who we lost

to cancer a few years ago.

My memories of my father will always be with me. My father was a

powerfully built man, with a broad chest and forearms like the barrel of

a baseball bat. His hair was as white as a blizzard, closely cropped in a

crew cut. My father never said a lot to me; but, growing up I always

could figure out whether he approved of my behavior or he didn't

approve of it. He had a glance; his eyebrows slanting inward, his steel

blue eyes blazing, his body tensing up like a cat ready to pounce, which

said forcefully and unequivocally to cease and desist. It was a menacing look. But if you were good, he had a completely different look. His body was relaxed and his smile stretched across the width of his face, as if to say welcome or congratulations. That look was comforting and inviting, like a warm, dry towel on the beach after a late September swim in the ocean. Dad's thoughts were painted on his face, right there in the open, never hidden, easy to interpret. This transparency made my life as a kid much less complicated, I always could figure out where I stood.

I remember when he took me to my first major league baseball game. I lived in New Jersey at the time; but we were visiting my grandmother, my mother's mom, who lived in the Mattapan section of Boston. I liked it there; we always ate Chinese food and I got to play with the local kids. While there on one visit, we took a trip to fabled Fenway Park. I will never forget that night. The grass was greener than I could have ever believed and there was that big green wall in left field with a scoreboard inside of it. I got a program, a souvenir cap, ate hot dogs and watched big fat Mickey Lolich of the Tigers pitch a shutout against the Red Sox. It was about as splendid as it gets for an eight year old boy.

I also remember a story Dad told me during that game. The telling of the story extended over several innings and dad was not an accomplished storyteller, but it was entertaining nonetheless. That story, and the animated way my father told it, also seemed to make that night even more special. Looking back, I think he told me that story to instill in me the sense that baseball occupies a prominent and unique place in American history. He wanted me to know that, as a kid, he had marveled at the awesome, magical spectacle of Major League Baseball, just like I was doing as I watched my first game and just like millions of other American kids had before me. It was a tall tale, a uniquely American tale, and a good one at that. It went something like this.

In 1951, New York City was blessed with three major league baseball teams: the New York Yankees, the Brooklyn Dodgers and the New York Giants. The Yankees, the class of the American League, won 98 games that year and won the pennant by five games. The National League was led by the other two New York teams, the Giants and the Dodgers, who both ended up tied at the end of the 154 game regular season, each with 96 wins, some 15 games better than their closest National League rival.

Never before and never since, had the three best teams on the face of the earth all resided in one place at one time, their ballparks within a short train ride of each other: Yankee Stadium in the Bronx; the Giants' Polo Grounds in Manhattan and the Dodgers' Ebbetts Field in Brooklyn. And my Dad was able to see games in every one of those parks that year, just by jumping on the subway train near his house in Queens, with his best friend Lefty Gerrig, and getting a seat in the outfield bleachers for a quarter.

It was an extraordinary year, perhaps the greatest baseball season ever played. There were essentially two subway series in 1951. Because the Giants and the Dodgers finished the season tied, they were required to engage in an extra best-of-three game showdown to determine the champion of the National League and to determine who would meet the Yankees in the World Series. And that three game set between the Dodgers and Giants became the most memorable, the most talked about, in Major League History.

The Giants won game one; the Dodgers evened it with a game two win. And game three, the all-time classic game, was punctuated by the famous walk-off three run home run by New York Giants outfielder Bobby Thomson, off Brooklyn Dodgers pitcher Ralph Branca, at the Polo Grounds in the bottom of the ninth inning. The Thompson homer, dubbed "The Shot Heard 'Round the World" gave the Giants a 5-4 victory. After 157 games, only one run separated these two great teams! To this day, over 50 years later, that home run is still cited as the most dramatic moment in Major League Baseball History. After that piece of theatre, the second Subway Series of 1951, which ended in Yankee victory over the Giants, was anti-climactic.

The Major League ballparks in those days were expansive, much larger than the dimensions of today's parks. It was not uncommon for the deepest part of centerfield to be as far as 480 feet from home plate. This required teams to place extraordinary athletes in centerfield, to insure hits would not slip between outfield gaps and to chase down fly balls. In 1951, the New York teams arguably had the three greatest center fielders ever, each one a Hall of Famer.

Joe DiMaggio, 1955 Hall of Fame inductee, played his last season in Centerfield for the Yankees in 1951. Joltin' Joe was an American Legend, the classic hero. Stylish and seemingly effortless on the field, Joe not only performed exquisitely, he looked superb doing it. DiMaggio was an icon even before he retired and was later immortalized to a new generation in the Simon & Garfunkle classic tune "Mrs. Robinson". Most of all Joe was a winner. How good was Joe DiMaggio? He played thirteen seasons for the New York Yankees and won ten American League pennants and nine World Series rings.

Willie Mays, 1979 Hall of Fame inductee, played his first season in Centerfield for the Giants in 1951. The "Say Hey Kid" was the National League Rookie of the Year in 1951 and went on to play over 20 more seasons in the Major Leagues. His bow legged gait was the antithesis of DiMaggio. Mays walked like an old man, seemingly struggling to take each next step. But it was all a ruse. In reality, Mays could do just about anything he wanted on the baseball field. In addition to hitting for average, hitting for power and stealing bases prolifically, Mays was the most spectacular fielder of all time. In fact, his over the shoulder catch in the 1954 World Series is generally regarded as the greatest fielding play ever made.

Duke Snider, 1980 Hall of Fame inductee, was already five years into his stellar career for the Dodgers in 1951. Of the three New York Centerfielders of 1951, Duke is the least appreciated. Yet in his first eleven seasons, he led the Dodgers to six pennants. Unlike Mays and DiMaggio, both right handed hitters, Snider hit from the left hand side of the plate. But like both Mays and DiMaggio, he was a well rounded player who could excel at anything on the baseball field. He had a cannon for an arm. And he had both power and speed; hitting more than 40 home runs in five consecutive seasons and prowling centerfield with grace and panache. When discussing the greatest centerfielders ever to play the sport, Duke Snider deserves strong consideration.

And in 1951 it was purely and simply a grand time to be a thirteen year old baseball fan and to live in New York. Outfield bleacher seats were so cheap you didn't need to mortgage your house just to see a game and, since the games were in the afternoon, you could even be home in time for supper, so you didn't have to get hassled by your older sister

Teresa. School was out in early June and by June 26, the Dodgers were in first place in the National League, five games ahead of the second place New York Giants. That day, June 26, 1951, my dad and his friend Lefty Gerrig decided to jump on the subway and take in their very first Major League Baseball Game. It would be at the Polo Grounds, between the New York Giants and the Brooklyn Dodgers.

The game was to start at 2:00, but Dad and Lefty wanted to get there early, to watch batting practice. They also figured that they could get a seat in the front row of the bleachers, right behind the Centerfielder, if they arrived first. The bleacher seats were the farthest from the action, but they were the only ones a thirteen year old kid from Queens could afford. And the sooner they got in line for tickets, the closer they would get to the action.

That morning, my Dad went over to Lefty's house, right next to the subway stop and banged on the door. "Hurry up, lets go!" he yelled. Lefty, just as eager to get going, grabbed his coat, sprinted down the stairs and through the door in a rush, yelling back to his mom, "See you tonight mom, I'm going out with Marty."

So at about 10:00 in the morning, the two friends got on a subway train in Queens, bound for Grand Central Terminal in Manhattan. They each had their baseball gloves in tow, eager perhaps to be lucky enough to catch a home run ball at the game. They made it to Grand Central Terminal, exited the train by 10:40 and hustled across the Main Concourse to get an Uptown train to the Polo Grounds, which was located North in the Washington Heights section of Manhattan. They would have no problem getting there by noon, when the box office opened. At 11:32, they exited the train and ran to the closest ticket window. They waited in line, fidgeting, as the clock ticked slowly towards 12:00. They had a good spot in line. They figured there were only about 100 fans in front of them, and not all of those fans would be vying for the prized front row seats in the bleachers.

At noon, the shade for the ticket window was raised and the line inched forward. When it was their turn, Marty and Lefty spit out their request. "Any front row bleacher seats out in Center?"

"You got the last two front row seats, boys; this is your lucky day. That'll be fifty cents, gentlemen," said the cashier.

And with that, the two boys each took a ticket and walked towards the bleacher entrance around the corner from the ticket window. They quickly moved through the turnstile and were handed their ticket stubs. This was great, they said to each other, beaming with delight.

When they arrived at their seats they noticed how sparse the huge park was. There was only a small smattering of people in the seats this early and very few players out on the field practicing yet. They noted the rookie Centerfielder for the Giants, Willie Mays, was shagging flies off the bat of one of his coaches. He was chattering as he chased down fly ball after fly ball and fired them back to one of the ball boys. "Say hey, give me a hard one coach, make me work. I want to show these kids why I'm in the Major Leagues." And Lefty and Marty loved it; cheering Willie wildly and screaming with glee as the rookie centerfielder glided all over the outfield making seemingly impossible catches with ease.

All at once, a fly ball came towards the center field wall, right in front of Lefty and Marty. In one motion, Mays reached out, caught the ball and whipped it back to his coach. "Damn," he said.

"What's wrong, Mr. Mays?" my dad blurted out.

"First off, I'm Willie, no Mr. Mays stuff with me, you guys. Second, I broke the web in my glove. I gotta get a new one in the clubhouse. I'll be right back out. Also, thanks for all the encouragement. We rookies need all the help we can get. What's your name?"

"Marty, and this is Lefty," Dad answered.

"First time at a Major League game?"

"Yeah, it's awesome," they answered together.

"I haven't seen too many games, myself. I just started playing here in May. But I aim on sticking here in New York a long time. I'm not going back to Birmingham," Willie said.

Willie continued, "Hey Kid, you want a souvenir of your first game? Take my old glove. I'll be right back."

And just like that, the great Willie Mays, maybe the greatest player who ever lived, tossed his old glove to my father and sped off to the dugout to get a new one. Willie could have well tossed up a bar of gold, as far as my Dad was concerned. He was much happier with that old glove; the glove of an actual Major Leaguer!

When Willie returned from the dugout, he continued to chatter while doing his pre-game workout. The boys were enthralled with Willie. What a great guy; so accessible, so enthusiastic and so upbeat. And when the game started, Willie continued his chatter. Willie made several outstanding plays in the field and after each one he yelled up to the boys in the stands, "How'd you like that one Marty?" or "Pretty good wheels huh, Lefty?" And Willie's outstanding fielding plays along with the pitching of Sal Maglie helped keep the Dodgers off the scoreboard that whole afternoon. As the game went on, the Giants scored in several innings, taking a 4-0 lead into the top of the eighth inning.

At this point in the story, my Dad told me that, in 1951, players left their mitts in the field when their team was batting. It was only in 1954 when the rules were changed; when players were required to remove their equipment, including gloves, from the field when their team was batting. So in the top of the 8th inning, all over the field of the Polo Grounds that afternoon, lay the mitts of the Brooklyn Dodgers; the gloves of legendary players such as Jackie Robinson, Gil Hodges, Roy Campanella, Pee Wee Reese, Carl Furillo and Duke Snider among them.

With two outs, Roy Campanella hit a long drive out toward the boys' new friend, the rookie Willie Mays. Willie sprinted to the warning path, right in front of Marty and Lefty, almost tripping over Duke Snider's glove. He caught the ball easily, just next to the wall separating the bleachers from the field. There were three outs. But, before he ran back to the dugout, Willie Mays mischievously grinned up at my Dad and said," Want another souvenir? Come and get it." He

37

then dropped the ball on the field, right next to Duke Snider's glove, tossed his own glove into left center field and ran to the dugout, chuckling.

As the players made their way in and out of the dugout, getting ready for the bottom of the inning, a thirteen year old boy named Marty jumped from the stands and quickly picked up that ball just dropped by Willie Mays. In his excitement, he also managed to scoop up the glove sitting next to the ball; the glove used that afternoon by Duke Snider. Dad hopped up and climbed back into the bleachers with the ball and glove in his hands. As he swung his foot over the wall, the ball dropped back onto the field, but he still had the glove; Duke Snider's glove. Lefty, in a panicked voice, said "Let's go Marty, before the Duke finds out!" And the two thirteen year old boys sped off, not waiting to see the end of their first Major League game, and sprinted immediately onto the subway. Because there were only a few people left in the bleachers, and because security in those days at the Polo Grounds wasn't so tight, the two friends were able to make a clean getaway.

Wow, what an afternoon, they thought, when they arrived home They saw their first Major League Baseball game, and also came away with two fantastic mementos from that game; the fielding gloves of the two centerfielders, Willie Mays and Duke Snider. The two friends agreed, this would be their secret. They did not ever want to be accused of stealing, so they had to keep quiet. In the case of Lefty, his Dad would whoop him beyond recognition if he ever knew what happened. And Marty did not want his sister to be faulted if he ever got caught. So Lefty put his ticket stub in Snider's glove and Marty put his ticket stub in Mays' glove. Then they wrapped up each glove in some old newspaper and placed the gloves in a brown paper bag in the corner of Marty's attic, behind the box where his sister hid the family's jewelry.

In the next few weeks, the boys got on the subway two more times to watch Major League Baseball games; once in Brooklyn and another time in the Bronx at Yankee Stadium. It was at the Yankee Stadium game that Marty came up with another idea.

"Lefty, we have Snider's glove and we have Mays' glove. Why don't we get DiMaggio's glove, too? Wouldn't it be neat to have the glove of each team's centerfielder? It would be a collection!"

"Marty, how are we gonna do that? That day with Willie Mays was once in a lifetime. Besides, how are we going to do the same thing here in Yankee Stadium? There are twice as many fans in the stands and there is security everywhere in this park."

"I'll come up with a plan, you'll see. Are you in?"

"This better be good Marty!" Lefty answered.

And so, while watching the Yankee game, deep in the bleachers of Yankee Stadium, my dad thought about hatching up a plan. It wouldn't be easy. It would have to be artful and clever. He would have to figure out the time when people were most distracted; when fans, umpires, players and ushers alike would overlook his presence. He would have to use sleight of hand distraction, like a magician.

40

As he watched the game, Dad studied DiMaggio. DiMaggio was not like Mays; he was silent and efficient, focused only on the game. He did not chatter much at all. He was all business; serious and aloof. He didn't speak to the fans. He seemed only to speak when calling off other outfielders from fly balls he was pursuing. Dad saw that Joe wanted to win above all else and figured he would be aggravated if a thirteen year old kid distracted him in any way. Dad knew he would get no cooperation from DiMaggio in this endeavor. He needed a new, very different strategy if he was to get DiMaggio's glove to complete the collection. He needed to study DiMaggio, the park and the rituals that took place during the game to figure this out.

The first thing my dad noticed about DiMaggio's routine was that when he went into the dugout between innings, he did not sit on the bench with his teammates. He disappeared down the runway to the clubhouse. That meant, unless it was near his turn to bat, DiMaggio wouldn't be watching if Dad slipped onto the field. DiMaggio also was the last Yankee to come out of the dugout and take his position in the field. Inning after inning, it was the same. He was always the last

41

player out of the dugout. These habits might give Dad more time to pick up the glove.

But, although DiMaggio's routine was conducive for the heist, the dimensions of the field and its layout were not. There was a chain link fence in the front of the bleachers closest to the point in right center field where DiMaggio seemed to always lay his glove when the Yankees hit. And the bleachers were high above the field; the drop from the bleachers to the field was too great. Dad would somehow have to find a way to sneak onto the field from the more expensive seats near the foul line in right field; where the seats were level with the field of play and the wall was waist level. If he wanted the glove, he would have to figure out a way to head out to centerfield from that point and still remain undetected.

The seventh inning stretch, the traditional interlude between the top and bottom of the seventh inning, was observed to be the best time to pull it off in my dad's estimation. Fans were talking, singing along to "Take Me Out to the Ball Game" or getting more refreshments. Ushers were focused on the stands where, by this time, some of the fans may have had a beer or two too many.

During the seventh inning stretch that night, Dad noted a ball boy chasing down some stray food wrappers that floated lazily onto the field. That would be it! He would sneak out onto the field in his pinstriped Yankee pajamas, disguised as a bat boy! The pajamas looked just like the uniforms worn by the batboys on the field. He would make sure some food wrappers drifted into right centerfield and, while cleaning up the field as a ball boy in disguise, swipe DiMaggio's glove. After Dad described the plan; Lefty agreed to help.

Lefty and Dad commenced devising their plan. They had to select an inconspicuous game. They scoured the schedule and decided on August 19, 1951. August 19 was a Sunday, the last game of a Yankee home stand. And it was also my dad's birthday; so that also might carry some good luck, if God were a baseball fan. And finally, the Yankees were to play the Philadelphia Athletics, a mediocre, sixth place team with no big stars. It seemed like the best choice; the safest choice.

When August 19th arrived, my father informed his sister that he would attend early morning mass because he intended to go to Yankee Stadium that afternoon with Lefty to celebrate his birthday. Shortly after returning from church, he rushed over to Lefty's house and they boarded the Subway. After a quick stop at Grand Central Terminal, they took the short subway ride up to Yankee Stadium. They didn't need to get the best seats this time. They just had to get into the ballpark. The plan was to go into the restroom near the lower tier of seats next to the right field foul pole in the fourth or fifth inning. Once there, Dad would change into his ball boy "uniform". Lefty would hold his street clothes and be responsible to make sure some food wrappers drifted into right centerfield just before the seventh inning stretch. Dad would quickly sneak down an aisle without an usher and slink onto the field. He would wait until the seventh inning stretch commenced and quickly swipe the glove. From there, it would be back up to the aisle, into the bathroom for a quick change and back onto the subway with Lefty, hopefully with DiMaggio's glove in their possession.

The boys took their customary seats in the bleachers, although there was no intention to sit there all afternoon. The game quickly became an aberration. The first place New York Yankees, the best team in baseball, were getting beat up all over the field by the lowly Athletics. It didn't matter who the Yanks put out on the mound; the Athletics were just better that day; smacking the ball all over the field. By the fifth inning, the score was Philadelphia Athletics 12, New York Yankees 1. Although disappointed with the Yankees' losing results, the boys noted that this unlikely performance might actually help their cause. Fans were clearing out all over the park, particularly in the seats in right field by the foul pole. Because of this, Lefty was able to sneak into one of those seats near the field; right near where DiMaggio was laying his glove each inning. His new seat would allow Lefty to toss the wrappers at just the right moment for Marty to proceed with the plan.

As the seventh inning approached, Dad snuck quickly down an aisle with no usher and dropped onto the field next to the tarp. He dropped down on one knee, striking a pose just like the ball boy close to the dugout. He looked around and no one did or said anything. Step one

45

was complete. He had gotten on the field, unnoticed. He would stay motionless in the same position, pretending he belonged in that spot. He looked like a ball boy to the crowd, ready to retrieve a ball if it came in his direction. His heart pounded as he looked up. Lefty, now sitting in a front row seat, nodded down at him holding up a cardboard box used to carry refreshments and some food wrappers.

Phil Rizzutto, the Yankee shortstop, threw out Eddie Joost to retire the Athletics in the top of the seventh. As soon as that last out was recorded, DiMaggio and Bauer, the right fielder, laid down their gloves and sprinted to the dugout. The organ started playing, to signify the start of the seventh inning stretch. Lefty then tossed the papers onto the field quickly; right next to DiMaggio's glove. In a flash, Dad sprinted out towards the refuse. When he reached the wrappers and cardboard container, he looked down and, there it was; the glove of the Great DiMaggio. Quickly Dad bent down, picked up the papers and ran back to foul territory. Curiously, he did not pick up the glove; although it was right there within his grasp and he could have gotten away with it. However, his conscience told him it was wrong. So the glove remained in its rightful place on the field and Dad snuck back to the men's room, meeting Lefty and changing quickly.

He looked at Lefty and said, "I couldn't. I just couldn't. It wasn't right." So the two boys went back to the bleachers and went home at the end of the game, which ended with a score of 15-1 in favor of the Athletics. End of story.

I laughed and said to my father sarcastically, "Good story. It's just like the story you told me about your scar from the German bayonet wound in World War II; you know, the scar which was actually from your appendix operation. I'm sure it really happened like that."

Dad answered, "No. You got me; it didn't actually happen just like that. Come on, you know I would never take anything that wasn't mine."

I interjected, "And you expect me to believe that Willie Mays would actually talk to a couple of kids like that? Give me a break." Even at eight years old, I was an inveterate cynic.

Notwithstanding the truthfulness of the tale, it made me smile and I am glad Dad told it to me. It showed that warm side of him; the entertaining and fun side. It was a good, affectionate memory, just the right kind of memory for this moment, as I made my way up the steps to see my Aunt Teresa for the last time in that house. We exchanged pleasantries and looked through old scrapbooks and yearbooks. My Dad was a great football player in High School and the clippings of his exploits were numerous. Teresa told me how proud she was of his achievements. As we continued to look over keepsakes, Teresa handed me several precious German Hummel statues that my father had sent her when he was in the army, stationed in Germany. It was good to sit and share these memories.

Then, she handed me an old dusty brown paper bag and told me to open it. She said that my dad placed this bag up in the attic a long time ago. Teresa said there was a story attached to the contents of the bag and that Lefty would be able to explain it better than her, if need be.

I opened the bag, reached in and pulled out an object wrapped in an old newspaper. I ripped off the newspaper, and found an old baseball glove. I quickly went to put my hand in the glove and noticed a ticket stub inside. It was a ticket to a baseball game between the New York Giants and the Brooklyn Dodgers at the Old Polo Grounds. The ticket was dated June 26, 1951. The Rawlings glove was inscribed on the inside of the pinky as follows: Duke Snider #4. I looked at the newspaper that was used as a wrapper, noting it was a page from a few days before the date on the ticket stub; the June 23, 1951 edition of the New York Post. Wow, could that story about Willie Mays actually be true?

I reached in and snatched another object which, just like the first, was wrapped in newspaper from the June 23, 1951 edition of the New York Post. Again, I stripped off the newspaper, revealing yet another baseball glove. This glove was a MacGregor model and the web was broken at the thumb. When I looked inside the wrist strap of the glove, there was a second ticket stub from the same game. I looked inside the glove for an inscription. Sure enough, in the palm of the glove, just under the pinky, was the inscription, Willie Mays. I gazed at Theresa with amazement, without saying a word. She said, "There's one more in the bag. Open it!"

I reached in and grabbed the third object, also wrapped in newspaper. The wrapping on this one was from the August 17, 1951 edition of the New York Post. When I opened it, I discovered a third baseball glove. This one was another Rawlings model and was in better shape than the other two. I looked inside the wrist strap and found two ticket stubs from a game on August 19, 1951 at Yankee Stadium, between the New York Yankees and Philadelphia Athletics. I looked inside the palm of the glove and noted the inscription: Joe DiMaggio #5. Wow, that old rascal!

"Theresa, Dad told me the story about the gloves. He said he didn't take DiMaggio's glove. He said he left it on the field. "

"No, he took it. And I wanted him to return them all. But I forgot about it after all these years. I found the bag in the attic last week. I was surprised he never did return those gloves. I guess that is for you to do now."

This collection of gloves was probably worth a fortune now, I thought. Collecting sports memorabilia is big business. I could make a nice financial windfall from this find. But the more I considered cashing in, the more I felt kind of sleazy, kind of dirty. These gloves were part of the golden age of baseball; when time moved slower, when baseball captured the imagination of a nation; when heroes like Willie Mays, Duke Snider and Joe DiMaggio could inspire us just by playing a kids' game. These gloves don't belong to my Dad. They don't belong to me. They don't even belong to Duke Snider, Willie Mays or Joe DiMaggio. They belong to all of us; to every American kid who ever journeyed to a Major League Ballpark and rooted for his team; his heroes. These gloves belong to the Hall of Fame. And that is where I intend to send them.

When I told Theresa of my intention, she smiled. She said she was proud of me.

Leaving West 71st

Leaving West 71st is a story of a yuppie natural gas trader who meets a musician, a union leader and a former President and has his life changed forever.

Leaving West 71st

Being invisible and indistinguishable can sometimes be a blessing. Escaping notice affords you the freedom to do things the way you want to do them, when you want to do them. Some people want to be rich and famous. As for me I'll just take rich; you can keep the famous part of it. Slipping under the radar, there are some people, places and things that just don't get any notice. Staten Island is like that. Staten Island is sometimes called the forgotten borough of New York City. Geographically isolated from the other boroughs, it sits outwardly separate and alone at the opening of New York Harbor, the first part of the City to welcome seafaring vessels. Though administratively part of the City, Staten Island is physically apart; not connected like the other four boroughs by the elaborate arteries that form the expansive subway transit system. It is however, distinctive and unique in its isolation because it is connected to Manhattan by the famous Staten Island Ferry. And a first-time ride on the Staten Island Ferry to Manhattan is a tremendous treat; giving the rider unrivaled water-views of the skyline of lower Manhattan, with the imposing Twin Towers perched straight ahead, and the glorious and inspiring Statue of Liberty and historic Ellis Island to the left. It is also the biggest bargain in my City. It has always been cheap, but since 1997 it is a free ride; and about 19 million passengers, some commuters and some tourists, take that ride every year. My Dad used to take that ride every day when he reported to work in Lower Manhattan. He took the ride for the efficacy of it, not so much to admire the view; it was simply the cheapest and fastest way to get to work.

I grew up in the Richmondtown section of Staten Island, which is occupied by mostly small split level homes built during the 1960s. Most of the people settled there to get away from the urban roughness of Brooklyn, in search of a more relaxed and suburban lifestyle. My mom was second generation Italian; my Dad third generation Irish and both were transplanted Brooklyn natives looking out for my future. My name is Brian Higgins and to this point I have done everything I was supposed to do in my life; always the dutiful, diligent son. I had a comfortable, but far from lavish middle class upbringing in

Richmondtown, with Dad working for many years maintaining the local natural gas pipes for the New York utility of Con Edison; and always providing the best he could for me and Mom. But Dad was tough, and he pushed me persistently to be the best I could be; that meant excelling in the classroom and on the hardwood. Life until my graduation from college consisted of three components: study, basketball and work. Sometimes I resented all the prodding and pushing, but in the end, all that effort seems to have paid off for me. I am now a twenty-eight year old single guy living in Manhattan in a great apartment on the Upper West Side. I make more money than I ever could have dreamed of as a kid and the new millennium signals bright hope and sanguinity for me.

I'm still in the family business, so to speak, only a very different side of it. I trade natural gas futures and options for the investment bank of Morgan Stanley in New York, located in the World Trade Center. Essentially, I get paid to watch a computer screen, kibitz with other traders and place bets on how natural gas prices will move; either up or down, based on all the disparate information I can gather. And I work hard; very, very hard at it. I live and breathe the natural gas market almost every hour of every day. I am constantly reading and gathering information about things that can affect the price of natural gas.

Trading natural gas is all about getting the best information you can and applying it to the bets you make. Trading successfully is defined as making as much money on your bets as possible; plain and simple. If you do that they pay you; they pay you a lot. Because of my fervor for trading successfully, and being paid a lot, I am now interested in all sorts of information that otherwise does not interest me the least bit; weather for instance. Weather used to be an influence in my life only to the extent it swayed such key life decisions as whether to wear flip flops or not. However, since severe weather directly impacts the demand for natural gas, I have freely and willingly become an amateur meteorologist, studying weather patterns incessantly, nerd-like. For example, if I see a cold front moving into the Midwest, apartments and office buildings in Chicago will need more heat, driving up demand for natural gas. Or if a hurricane hits the Gulf of Mexico, it will affect supply by shutting down the platforms that move the gas into the pipelines from under the water. I also now fervently study such compelling dynamics as the price movements of other energy related commodities like oil, electricity and coal, as well as the relationship of the US Dollar to other world currencies. That is a completely different mess of factors to assess, with domestic politics, international politics and overall general economics all entering into the stew of factors to mentally savor.

But most important of all, trading often just comes down to trying to guess what the other traders are doing and exploiting their miscues for my own benefit. Sometimes the markets do not move logically; however, so even though I have a great deal of high-quality information, I still sometimes lose. There are a lot of natural gas traders down in Houston who can move markets just by increasing the volume of their bets. That creates momentum in the market that defies logic and prices subsequently move illogically.

A lot of those traders work for a huge company in Houston named Enron; which I and my colleagues not so affectionately refer to as the Evil Empire. The Enron traders are noted as particularly cold-blooded in an industry noted for cold-bloodedness. At Enron, being ruthless is their calling card, their company raison d'etre. Employees collectively revel in the swashbuckling, damn the rules culture and wear it as a badge of honor; kind of like a Mafia family comprised entirely of devious MBAs. I even thought of joining the dark side once, but quickly dismissed that thought, realizing in one of my more lucid moments that the only culture in Houston is yogurt. I have a life-sized cardboard cutout of Darth Vader attached to the wall behind my desk with the Enron company logo on his chest. We throw darts at Darth after the market closes each day for amusement. If you hit Darth in the target between his legs with a dart, in the precise place that causes most gentlemen concentrated and extreme pain, you win the office pool.

Natural gas trading is a great job because it is truly just a game, like when I played basketball in college. Every day you compete hard and every day you either win or lose. When I win I have fun; an awful lot of fun. My scorecard is tallied in terms of dollars made or dollars lost. If I do well and make money for the firm I will get my own wheelbarrow full of money, and a six or even seven figure bonus at year end. However, if I consistently lose money for the firm I will lose my job. So much depends upon that scorecard of mine; so much depends upon a red wheelbarrow, filled with money.

My dad doesn't understand any of this. He rants, "How can a twenty-eight year old kid get a six figure bonus when the most I ever got after forty years at my job was a handshake, some useless S&H green stamps, a watch I didn't want and a departure bonus of a thousand dollars? Also, I can't understand how your job is actually producing anything of value for anybody. The gas gets pumped out of the ground by some guys working down in New Orleans or Houston. And it gets pushed through a pipeline that is maintained by crews of hard hats working for big utility companies along the pipeline. Why don't the guys actually getting dirty get the six figure bonuses? They are the ones doing the work. All you are doing is placing bets, just like I do when I lay down $20 on the Jets game every Sunday or go play the ponies. They pay you for that? And besides, all that speculation you guys do just drives the prices up for people like me who really work for a living."

Alas, I tell him, it is capitalism at work and thank you as always, Dad, for the heartfelt words of encouragement. I went to Dartmouth, got my Columbia MBA in 1997 and then impressed the folks at Morgan

Stanley just enough to get this job. Is Dad not a tad arrogant to question the wisdom of the marketplace? If Morgan Stanley feels my job merits a six figure bonus, then I am not about to argue that point, and neither should he. Take the money and be thankful. Perhaps I should give Dad a copy of Adam Smith's writings for next Christmas. Or perhaps not; Dad would probably think the book was about his favorite superheroes, Batman and Robin; confusing Adam Smith with Adam West was a distinct possibility in Dad's case. Dad was the consummate Batman fan and he always searches the obscure cable stations looking for the classics from his self-designated Golden Age of Television such as "Batman", "Green Acres", and "Banacek", which featured his favorite actor, the gifted thespian George Peppard.

Anyways, I had another great day today. My ledger increased by over $4.5 million. Everything clicked. The winter of 2001 has been one of the coldest on record in the Northeast, natural gas inventories have been depleted throughout the winter and inventories remain well below normal levels for this time of year. As a result, futures prices have risen dramatically from when I placed many of my bets last summer. My positions have been net long during this period, meaning I bet on an increase in natural gas prices. The market has obliged me; my guesses have worked out perfectly. So, as I leave my desk and head home tonight, I survey the Majesty of New York Harbor from my perch on the 74th Floor, blow a kiss to the Statue of Liberty and think to myself that life is definitely good. I am not going to do any research tonight on my computer. I'm going home to my apartment on 71st Street and curl up on the couch with a Ray's Pizza and a Heineken, and watch the New York Knicks on television.

Back home, I have my pizza and beer and watch the game, which turns out to be a low scoring, nail biter. No more than five points separate the Knicks from the Miami Heat over the entire game. And with three seconds left, the score at 76-74 in favor of the Knicks, Tim Hardaway of the Heat barely misses a three point shot as the buzzer sounds and time elapses. We have a Knick win. In the signature word of the peerless Knicks broadcaster Marv Albert, Yes! And on that note I roll off my sofa, change into pajamas, turn off the lights, crawl into bed and close my eyes; a great ending to an overall great day.

Soundly and happily I sleep, until I am awakened abruptly. Hearing a man speaking nonsense slowly to me in a melodic, almost song-like, voice with a familiar British accent, I wonder. Is it a dream or has a homeless vagrant flown over from London for the sole purpose of wandering into my apartment and boorishly waking me up from a sound and comfortable sleep? I suppose it is a dream, since, after surveying the apartment, it is clear that nobody is here but me. I could go right back to sleep, but I am strangely intrigued by the British accent of the narrator; the nonsensical hodgepodge of words still hopping around in my head.

"Come have dinner with your father of state.

Whatever, whatever, whatever's your fate.

Laugh, smile and talk for a while.

Eat, think and drink in colonial style.

Find a pearl on the corner of Broad.

Listen to us and prepare to be awed.

In the room named for dad with the curly white rug.

When you figure it out, go and ask for the bug."

I have heard that voice before, yet I cannot attach it to anyone in particular. I can dismiss this all as meaningless fertilizer and resume my sleep, but I have always thought the dream-state is when our minds are the least burdened and most open to other dimensions and new ways of thinking; at least that is what my freshman literature professor told me at Dartmouth. So, even though it is 3:00 a.m., I decide to document the verse and see if it will make sense at breakfast. Now out of my bed, I slide across the hard wood floor, to sit in the club chair next to the bedroom window. Quickly I write down the words recited in my dream. Sitting in the chair writing the dream-verse, I gaze down at the street below. Although I live in the city that never sleeps, chilly Tuesday nights in February are generally still and quiet here on West 71st and Broadway. The Hudson's cold wind, channeled toward Central Park through the ravine formed by the soaring buildings on either side of 71st Street, puts a shroud over the usual revelry of the street scene.

I look out the window eastward, toward Central Park, and am immediately startled by an implausible stream of light that shines up into the sky from the street several blocks away. Like a light-beam from a lighthouse, it emanates upward from the street; its source unidentifiable, translucent like fog and moving straight up, not

wavering right or left, just climbing rapidly into the heavens. I stare at

the beam, transfixed. Then, after a minute or two, the beam abruptly

ceases. I stare for several more minutes to see if the light will resume

its ascent, yet am disappointed. I note nothing. It is gone as quickly as

it came.

What could that light have been? It was undeniably dramatic and

startling. But in New York City, dramatic and startling things happen

every day. Was it a UFO or just some stupid publicity stunt for some

new dandruff shampoo or Broadway Musical about aliens invading the

Bronx? Maybe it was simply a powerful light from a Con Edison

utility truck. I guess I will be able to find out what it was tomorrow; if

it is anything at all. With the light gone, there looks like nothing more

to see; it is time to crawl back into bed. So I curl up and drift back to

sleep, thankful for a few more hours of rest before I must head back to

work in the morning.

About two hours later, I am awakened by the music on my alarm clock;

an old Beatles song blares. "Let me take you down, 'cause I'm going to Strawberry Fields, nothing is real and nothing to get hung about. Strawberry Fields forever." I shut off the alarm; it is now 5:45 a.m., Wednesday, February 21, 2001. I walk toward the bathroom past my telephone answering machine and notice the light blinking, indicating that someone has left me a phone message. Odd, because there were no messages when I went to sleep and I did not hear the phone ring overnight. Quickly I play the phone message and am surprised to hear the voice on the message; the same voice as in the strange dream from last night and now he is singing, picking up the Beatles song exactly where it left off when I turned off the radio, singing the next verse. "Living is easy with eyes closed, misunderstanding all you see. It's getting hard to be someone, but it all works out. It doesn't matter much to me."

Weird and a little eerie, I think, now recognizing the voice; it sounds just like John Lennon. It is a spot-on imitation actually; impeccable in its simulation of the tone, inflection and accent of the master love guru/musician from the 1960s and 1970s. Whoever left that message is either an incredible impressionist or some kind of clairvoyant like John Edwards who is channeling Lennon. I wonder if maybe someone down

66

at the office is messing with my head. In any case, I need to get ready for work; I have to trek downtown on the subway to 2 World Trade Center for another day of trading. So I head to the shower and get ready.

Before I leave, I pour myself a bowl of cornflakes and milk; and eat the last slice of cold pizza from last night. For the aghast and uninformed, as a bachelor living alone in Manhattan, it is appropriate and culturally acceptable for me to do things like eat cold pizza with my cornflakes or to sit on the leather couch in my living room in only my underpants, as long as I do these things only in my own place, either alone or in front of my college buddies. So as I finish the pizza, I pore over the message from last night's dream, unsure about what most of it means. Who or what is the father of state or the pearl on the corner of Broad? But I am struck by the last line. "When you figure it out, go and ask for the bug." A beetle is a bug and John Lennon is a Beatle! If this dream means anything at all, it probably has something to do with John Lennon or the Beatles!

I would love to figure the rest of this out, though. It's a puzzle; a dream-poem of allusions that is challenging me to decode it. I always thought it odd that poets would fill their works with vague references designed for academics to spend hours debating and deliberating. But trying to figure out this verse is actually a fun little personal challenge. That poetry class in college, with all those scholarly pinheads looking for meaning in all those meaningless lines, may finally be of use after all. That class taught me how to open my mind's eye to clues and meanings that only exist inside me. Well enough of that malarkey, I think, as I grab my coat. I need to catch a train to work.

As I ride the subway downtown, my thoughts are again back where they should be, on the natural gas market. Prices are strong and it is cold, but I have an inkling prices will not be so strong through the summer. But it is just a feeling at this point. I need to get a better feel for the market today, to gather some news and hype, to see if my hunch has validity. When I get to my desk, I have a message waiting for me in my voicemail; its John Lennon again. "Brian, people matter; be someone. Look inside your heart and mind and live. The straight line isn't always the most efficient path; don't be afraid to change. Go short all summer and then be done with this gig. If you do, you will make a lot of money. After that, spend the rest of your time and money on what matters, on your joy and passion. Something will happen in September that will pain you and many others. Profit from the heartache and move on. All you need is love. Bye."

After hanging up the phone, I look over at Linc, the guy who sits next to me in the trading pit. Linc's given name is Nigel Lincoln Allbridge III, an honest to goodness WASP with blood bluer than Yankee pinstripes. His dad is on the executive committee of the firm and Linc is ostensibly learning the ropes so that he can pretend he worked his way up the ranks before he has his coronation to the Executive Committee. Linc stands as tall as me at 6'4'' and has light blond, almost white, hair; with white teeth, white skin and white shoes to match. In fact, everything about Linc is white; and preppie. From his L.L. Bean argyle sweater/loafer sets to his Absolut gin and tonics to his subscription to The Wine Enthusiast and his top of the line Mercedes, Linc radiates money to everyone around him. One notable thing I have come to learn in life is that people with money; with boatloads of old world, inherited money like Linc, never go by their first name. They always go by their middle name to avoid confusion with their prominent father or grandfather or uncle and most of them need to have a wealth-inspired nickname like Chip, Jay or Tad. Curiously, the nickname fascination is one of one of the few things moneyed WASPs have in common the rest of us and with more familiar proletarian groups like the mafia ("Vinnie the Brow", "Joey Fat", "Johnny Boo Boo" and "Tony Braziole") and rappers ("Lil' Pimp J", "Biggie Shrimps", "Fug Dawg" and "Bump Da Benz").

I met Linc at Columbia, and despite his aura of entitlement and privilege, he actually isn't a bad guy; we get along pretty well. And because of the prominent position his dad occupies, other traders are constantly trying to curry favor with him, to kiss his proverbial hind quarter; whispering their best information to him, hoping he, as well as they, profit from it. So Linc gets a lot of information, and because we are friends, he will be forthcoming when we talk. "Where do you think prices are going?" I ask Linc.

"It is a tough market to call right now, Brian. It could go either way; but I think down in the long-term. Natural gas is now over $8 a decatherm. Oil prices are lower right now, and gas production is strong. So the dual fuel users will use oil rather than natural gas. Plus the cold weather in the East usually means a mild hurricane season. I think gas inventories will pop up this summer causing prices to fall. What do you think?"

All I can think of is the voice of John Lennon; go short all summer and be done with this gig. That ethereal advice, coupled with Linc's concise, logical analysis, convinces me to throw caution into the wood chipper and bet the ranch on a big price drop "I agree. I'm shorting my whole book as much as they let me through November. I know I'll win." My voice was full of bravado. It is always good to look decisive in front of the guy who may some day be running the show. But it wasn't just bluster, I felt like I knew something, I felt strong about that now. I felt just like my Dad did many years ago, one day at the track at Aqueduct; when he happened to have the good fortune to run into our neighbor, Mr. Finnegan, who was an FBI agent. Dad was looking at the program when he felt a tap on the shoulder. It was Finnegan. Without saying a word, Finnegan took the program out of Dad's hands. Turning the pages, Finnegan circled a 100-1 long-shot in the eighth race, a 50-1 long-shot in the ninth race and another 100-1 long-shot in the tenth race. He then walked off without even a word or a nod to Dad. So, even though those horses were all long-shots, Dad bet $20 on each of them. And he walked out of the track that day with $5,000. And neither Finnegan nor Dad ever spoke of the incident for over twenty years; Dad finally broke his silence only after Mr. Finnegan passed away a few years ago, at Finnegan's wake.

Linc responded, "You know the guys at Enron are pushing the price up now; so we are going against the market, but I agree with you, the market has been so strong this winter there is nowhere to go but down. I'm with you." Bold and ballsy; I'm going to love working for this guy someday.

Because the Enron guys were looking to push prices up, we were able to make our big bets without immediately influencing the market downward at all. We were able to get all our bets off at nice high prices. So, on February 21, 2001 with natural gas trading around $8.00 per decatherm, we both layed down our bets; big, huge bets of over 50 million decatherms each month, April through November 2001; all short, all betting that prices will fall. And after that day both Linc and I stopped actively trading. We just sat and waited for the price of natural gas to fall. And fall it did; all summer. The Inside FERC price for each of the summer months was as follows: April Inside FERC price- $5.33, May Inside FERC price- $5.32, June Inside FERC price- $4.13, July Inside FERC price- $3.62, and August Inside FERC price- $3.63. Both Linc and I each individually make over a billion dollars for the firm in just those few months. At those numbers, even if I just break even the rest of the year, I will get an eight figure bonus, more than $10 million. Dad might really take notice of those numbers. Maybe I'll throw the old coot a bone like a swimming pool or a new car, just to express some overdue gratitude and show him my job actually means something.

So thanks to some prescient analysis on Linc's part and my hunch about my ghostly prognosticator, Linc and I have a great summer. We spend our weekdays mimicking the sound of cash registers shouting "Ka-ching, Ka-ching" over and over again; and we spend our weekends on the beach in Southampton, learning how to surf, eating a whole lot of lobster and drinking a whole lot of Heineken. We had rented a big house a short walk from the beach and because we had no work worries, we just plain enjoyed ourselves. We closed it all out on Labor Day, with a big barbeque at the House to celebrate our good fortune before our crew heads back to Manhattan, poised to continue our mastery of the markets.

Interestingly, I haven't heard that British voice since February, when it predicted the downward spiraling natural gas market for me. I was hoping for a few more tips, but none were forthcoming. Even though my run of luck was spectacular, my hunger for more money-making was not yet satisfied. I want tips, tips and more tips. But when I get back to my apartment at about 11:00 p.m. that night after the Labor Day Barbeque, I have another message on my answering machine. It is the John Lennon voice singing. "Living is easy with eyes closed; misunderstanding all you see. It's getting hard to be someone but it all works out. Open up your eyes and see." Strawberry Fields Forever, again, changed a little in its words; but no market tips. Oh well, I have work tomorrow morning and it is time for bed.

Next day begins as do most work days; shower, get dressed, eat breakfast and take the subway downtown. When I reach my desk at about 7:00 a.m., I have a message in my voice mailbox from the mysterious Mr. Lennon. "Don't eat lunch at your desk today, go out and get some fresh air." I always eat lunch at my desk; the Company brings around a menu to order from at about 11:00 a.m. and a messenger delivers what you order to your desk. Management wants you at your desk all day long looking at the computer screen, trading molecules of gas back and forth with the other folks sitting at their desks all day long looking at their computer screen, trading molecules of gas back and forth. But I have made so much money for the firm over the last few months that I can pretty much call my own shots and do what I want now. If I want to go out for a few hours, no one is going to stop me; after all I am now the biggest producer in the place a this point, due in no small part to my mystic soothsayer Mr. Lennon. Maybe I will meet the guy and get more tips. So today I will go out for lunch. I'm hoping if I follow the directives of the voice, maybe I will get a few more savory market tips. So when noon time rolls around, I leave the building, head down as I shuffle through the crowd, and wonder where I should go to get lunch. While I am thinking, smack, I bump right into two people, a man and a woman. The man speaks, "Sorry sir. We are from out of town and have reservations to eat at Fraunces Tavern. Can we trouble you for directions?"

"Oh, sure, no problem. It's on Pearl, on the corner of Broad. I'll walk you guys over that way. You guys from out of town?"

The woman spoke, "Yes from Ann Arbor, Michigan; this is our first time to New York and it is wonderful. We are here on vacation; we are both huge history buffs; we are really looking forward to lunch at Fraunces Tavern. We visited the Cloisters yesterday, Rockefeller Center this morning and we are heading out to the Statue of Liberty this afternoon after lunch. This is a really, really nice trip."

I have been past Fraunces Tavern hundreds of times, but I have never stopped in there. Now I thought to myself why hadn't I? These out-of-towners were in New York for the first time and were going to have lunch at this famous historical tavern; where General Washington, the father of our country, and the other Sons of Liberty planned their succession from the tyrannical British and where in 1783, General

Washington bade his final farewell to his loyal generals after their improbable victory. Fraunces Tavern at 54 Pearl Street, Manhattan's oldest surviving building was reportedly George Washington's favorite watering hole in all the colonies. As I walked the tourists into the door of the tavern, that familiar voice bellowed to me and a man with long hair and glasses reached out and shook my hand as he spoke.

"Brian, so glad to meet you in the proverbial flesh after all these months; even though I personally have no flesh anymore. John, John Lennon." I froze. John Lennon has been dead for twenty years! I must have turned white because John continued, laughing, "What's the matter Brian? You look like you've seen a ghost. Ha. Well, very funny lad, I suppose you have! Get this, I'm a ghost and you are the only one here who can see me; so listen well; don't gesture or anything right now or they will think you're crazy. Next Saturday night, I and a couple of the boys from the other side are having dinner here in the Washington Room after the place closes. Show up here at about 12:30, knock on the door and ask for me, the Bug, or Bugsy if you like; that's what my new friends call me nowadays. Ah, it's great to be back in

77

New York, my favorite town in the whole world. So I'll see you then, Brian?"

I pause. "Okay," I mutter lowly, quite unsure of myself.

"Great, get out of here now. Go back to your computer screen and do your little trading thing with all the other little traders. I'll see you here Saturday night."

After that interaction, I am in a bit of a fog and the week rushes by. My short positions continue to throw off gobs of profit, but I don't seem to care anymore; I am utterly distracted. I have seen a ghost- literally, and all I can think about is Saturday night. Is this real or am I seeing things? Am I crazy or am I sane? Am I blessed or am I cursed?

My mind races all week until Saturday night finally rolls around. I get on the train to go downtown and expect to get there right around 12:30. As I come up to the street out of the subway I am struck at how much more deserted Downtown Manhattan is on the weekend. The streets get a respite from the throngs of racing workers and gawking tourists that clog their passages during the week. As I make my way towards the tavern, I see a light beam just like the one I saw in February, when I wrote down the dream-verse.

And now the verse is clearer; I am to eat in the Washington Room, hence the references to the father of state, and Fraunces Tavern is on the corner of Pearl and Broad and is noted for its colonial inspired cuisine. It actually now makes sense. As I arrive at 54 Pearl Street, I note that it looks closed. I reach out, knock on the door and softly say, "I'm here to see the Bug."

The door opens and I am greeted by a tall distinguished, but eerily familiar-looking gentleman dressed in colonial garb. He has thinning reddish brown hair, tied back in a short pony tail. He reaches out, shakes my hand and says, 'Brian, pleased to meet you. Glad you could join us tonight. We'll be dining upstairs with John Lennon and Peter McGuire. I am your host this evening. My name is George Washington." Holy Father of Our Country, Batman; that is the face on the dollar bill! As we walk up the stairs he continues in a relaxed, easy-going tone, "What ale do you fancy? I like the new stuff you young folk drink, named after my old friend Sam Adams. I recommend it highly."

"Cool," I mutter without knowing what to say, "I'll have a cold Sam Adams too."

When we reach the Washington Room I see two others seated in front of a table filled with food and drink; with lamb, beef, oysters, scallops, pot roast and all varieties of vegetables. A second table is filled with pies of all varieties, apple, blueberry, peach and cranberry. It all smells heavenly. Lennon is at the table eating with another man who I do not recognize. "Sit down. Do you know who these guys are?" Washington asks. Without missing a beat he continues, "Oh sure, you know Bugsy, the other fellow is Peter McGuire. Pete, why don't you tell Brian about yourself while we eat?"

"I'm Peter McGuire and like these other two guys, I really enjoy a good ale; so I guess we're all going to drink Sam's tonight. Where do I start? Real quick, I was born in 1852 in Manhattan and lived here on and off most of my life. I had to quit school at 11 to support the family when Dad went off to fight in the War Between the States. I was good with my hands so I made ends meet as a carpenter and piano maker. Working in Manhattan at that time I believed us workers didn't get our fair share; so I stood up and let people know how I felt. Somehow I got mixed up in the Union movement. Even though I was only about twenty years old, I became a pretty well known spokesperson for the movement and eventually started the United Brotherhood of Carpenters and later the American Federation of Laborers. That was pretty heady stuff for a kid with little formal education; but I was able to connect with the immigrants of the day. They believed in what I said and so did I. In 1883, I led a festive parade of workers through the streets of Manhattan on the first Monday of September. That was one of the few parades we staged in the early days that the cops didn't beat the stuffing out of us; it was really nice to just do something we believed in and not have to pay for it with our blood. That parade lead to more parades of the like on that day each year, all over the country. Several years later, Congress made Labor Day an official Holiday. So you have me to thank for that Lobster Barbeque, Brian."

"Things haven't changed that much though have they Pete," Lennon commented. "The guy who actually creates something, a product or service still doesn't get the reward."

"Yeah, but at least now the worker gets a living wage. Things are better. I believe I helped in that regard. At the end of my life I felt that way; John, I was discouraged and depressed, I drank too much. That did nobody any good. But now I look back and am proud. I mean, I could have continued just making pianos and done okay financially; but instead I stood up for my beliefs and did my best to make things better."

Washington interjected with a laugh, "Bugsy, you little Marxist scalawag, lighten up; always thinking about the classes and the masses. Let's raise our glasses! And Bugsy, kiss all our asses!"

"George, you want to kiss this fist?" Lennon asked agitated.

"Ha, I was just kidding, John. Besides, as history has aptly documented, I have had pretty good luck in my spats against you Brits.

Come on now, we're good friends; let's lighten up a bit. You guys want to jam, now? Brian, you play bass right? John has rhythm guitar, I have drums. Pete has piano. Let's have some fun."

I looked over and there, magically, appeared microphones, speakers, a piano, a drum set and two guitars. Lennon brightened up and strutted over, saying, "Hard Days Night on four. One, two three, four." Lennon hit the opening chord and everyone followed, perfectly in sync. I joined right in with the other three. As you would expect, Lennon was phenomenal, but Washington and McGuire were very accomplished too and the band sounded great together. We did a whole set of rocking numbers, "Twist and Shout", "I Wanna Hold Your Hand", "Help" and a whole slew of Beatles songs .

Finally McGuire said, "We have to leave soon; time is fleeting; daybreak will be upon us soon. John, could you play "Imagine" that's my favorite."

Peter stood up and John quickly hopped over to the piano and started to play. The music was beautiful and the words were as touching as the first time I heard that masterpiece. Lennon sang with such poignancy, in his words and in his soulful, heartfelt singing. And when it was done we all clapped. Lennon looked right at me and said, "Brian, Monday morning call your boss and tell him you can't make it to work this week. Make up whatever excuse you need to. On Monday, go to the Statue of Liberty and Ellis Island. And drink it all in; enjoy your heritage. On Tuesday, get on the 8:45 a.m. Staten Island Ferry and go see your Mom and Dad. And stay with Morgan Stanley only until you get your bonus in December. It will be bigger than your wildest dreams. And in December, after you receive the bonus money, think of me, Peter and George and what ever happens between now and December. Think hard about these things and follow your passion. And make the world better."

I then spoke, "I would be entirely remiss if I were not to thank each of you for tonight. It was great fun. Wow, I am in the presence of true greatness. I hope someday I will again have the pleasure of seeing you three and playing with you."

Lennon spoke again, "That is entirely up to you and what direction you decide to go in December."

And with that, a bright light emanated from the floor and lifted the three ghosts up in a flash. The light was so bright I briefly had to close my eyes. And when I opened my eyes, I stood alone. Only I was no longer in the Washington Room at Fraunces Tavern, but in my own living room on West 71st Street. The time on the clock was 12:30 a.m., exactly the time I arrived at the Tavern. It was as if the night had not happened at all. I was tired and so I turned in to bed.

And on Monday morning I called into work, letting them know I had to take the week off. I rode out to the Statue of Liberty on that beautiful Monday morning. As I arrived at Liberty Island, I admired the graceful statue, holding its torch out to welcome all the visitors, its bronze body made green from the elements. With the others who accompanied me on the ferry out to the Island, I climbed to the top of Lady Liberty and enjoyed the spectacular view. And I looked around me; everyone was smiling, relishing their visit to this stupendous landmark. I saw faces of all ages, young and old and faces from all over the world, speaking languages I had never before heard. Next, I continued on to Ellis Island and I spied the names of my paternal great grandparents on the list of immigrants who came through the looking glass to this country, through this famous entry point. And I was proud and humbled at the same time. I spent the whole day out at those two landmark islands. And I thought to myself how great my city and my nation are; and how blessed I have been to live here. And I went home that night kind of bewildered; kind of ashamed that I had not sacrificed like all those people who came to America or fought for some ideal bigger than myself like John Lennon, Peter McGuire and George Washington did. And I thought Lennon's suggestion to see Mom and Dad tomorrow was a good one; to take the ferry like Dad had all those years and go home. I needed to say thank you again to them for what they gave me; opportunity.

I woke up the next morning and went for an early jog through Central Park. It is a warm September day, the sun shines brightly, warming me as I weave through the paths of the park. After cleaning up, I take the same subway line as I usually do when I go to work; only today I am going to visit Mom and Dad on the ferry. It is Tuesday morning,

September 11, 2001, a warm and gorgeous day; one of those Indian summer beauties that only come around a few times each year. I board the ferry and we depart promptly as scheduled at 8:45. I am going against the traffic; the morning ferry is packed with commuters to Manhattan, but only sparsely filled with folks visiting Staten Island. As we roll off the docks I look up at my workplace and think of my friend Linc and all the good times we had this summer. And then something odious happens. An airplane flies directly into the next building, One World Trade Center. 'Oh my God," a woman screams. "How could that be? What a terrible accident!"

The back of the boat fills and is now crowded as the passengers stare at the calamity. As we pull away, I watch the fire and smoke billow from the tall building. No one says anything. It is eerily quiet. We are all stunned, staring back at Manhattan, looking at the flames starting to emanate from the skyscraper. We stare for several minutes until the unthinkable then happens; a second plane flies into Tower Two. And now I know, it is no accident, it is terrorism; it has to be. The World Trade Center was targeted by terrorists in 1993 and this is the evil encore. I said a lengthy and heartfelt prayer for all the people in the buildings: for my friend Linc; for Leon, who used to bring me my lunch every day; for Oliver, who used to come and shine our shoes for a buck two times a week and for all the others I saw each and every day. We sometimes take it all for granted; our blessings, our city and our country. I said another prayer silently as the boat powered on.

The boat continued for about eight minutes after the second plane hit. As we pulled into the dock at St George in Staten Island, I knew my life needed to change. And I was determined to change it; to start making a difference to someone other than myself. I quickly hailed a cab and rode out to see my Mom and Dad. I still had my key to the house; so I let myself in. My parents were in the living room; silently watching the buildings burn on the television. Without saying a word, I grabbed Mom and hugged her for about a minute. Then I went to my Dad and hugged him; hugged him like I never had before, with sincere, heartfelt love and gratitude. A tear came down his face. I had never seen my Dad cry before. "Dad," I said, "I'm gonna make you proud of me."

In the remaining months of 2001 many things happened. The World Trade Center became known as Ground Zero, after the buildings there all collapsed; and although most of my colleagues were spared, my friend Linc, who I thought had everything, lost his life. I attended his and several other funerals; funerals of young men and women who died before their time for no other reason than they were working that day. The Statue of Liberty closed; you can no longer enter her body and make the long inspiring climb to her summit, her flame. And Enron, the Evil Empire, passed on, victim of its own malevolence, when it declared bankruptcy on December 4th.

I took my bonus check of $42 million that December, made sure it cleared, and resigned shortly thereafter. The firm pressed me hard; hoping to persuade me to stay. I spoke to several members of the Executive Committee, including the Chairman of the firm; and each one gave me a litany of reasons why I should continue with the firm. Their reasons for staying around were all sound and rational from an economic perspective. But none of their reasons addressed how staying would make me happy, or how my staying impacted anyone but me. I have always done what was expected of me; now it is time to live, to take a chance and do the unexpected. As I leave, I don't know where I am going. But I want to play again someday with Lennon, Washington and McGuire. With them as my inspiration I am sure I will land somewhere amazing.

The Keeper of the Light

The Keeper of the Light is a story of faith and renewal set in the Depression.

The Keeper of the Light

Nothing makes you lose your moral compass like money. That seems so obvious to most, but at this point in my life that obvious notion is drowning me, sapping me of my zeal. I know of terrible, reprehensible things that are overlooked; pain and suffering that is ignored, all for the interests of money. A stage mother allows her daughter to fall prey to a pedophile; just so her daughter gets the lead in a Broadway play. A wealthy contractor pays kickbacks to customers to drive his smaller competitors out of business. A well heeled Wall Street honcho pads his already bursting pockets with insider trades. A prominent district attorney accepts a bribe from an organized crime figure to allow a "problem", a live human being, to disappear somewhere, never to be found. I know of all these things, because I hear them all in the confessional. I hear them more often than I care to.

I am bound by duty to never tell these things; yet I am conflicted by that duty. Will these pretenders, these nastiest elements of humanity, ever be held accountable? It seems like an awful long time to wait for judgment day; too long a time before they are sentenced. If I could stop these things from happening now, isn't that better than just listening idly behind this confessional screen? If I absolve them now, am I not just part of the problem? And what if I don't absolve them? There is always the possibility that they are actually repentant. How can I tell if they are sorry? Who am I to judge what is in their hearts in the first place!

But money matters become particularly perplexing when you are charged with overseeing financial stability for the Archdiocese; effectively charged with raising as much money as possible, never questioning the source; while simultaneously moralizing for your flock to follow the Word. I feel torn and conflicted; serving two seemingly opposite and meaningless contradictions at once. I am becoming disgusted and disillusioned with my own life. I am, for the first time, questioning my mission of the last forty years. Yet, I sense that I am trapped; I can see nowhere else to go but to trudge forward. I am the Cardinal; the leader of the New York Archdiocese; the most visible Catholic in the United States. They call me the "Cardinal of Charity" because of my skill at raising and administering funds for the Church. If I leave this post for something more to my liking, I feel it would send a dreadful message; it would admit my spiritual defeat. I have a duty to God, the Church and to my family to forge ahead, even if the joy in doing so has already left me; even with my spirit broken and weary.

When I was twenty one years old, things were simpler. Everything could be summed up in the following words: I have the calling. Everything was lucid and understandable; good and bad; black and white. My aunt, who came to New York from Ireland and raised me after mother's death, was so full of pride; so full of bliss. Patrick has the calling! She never got tired of repeating that phrase. I would be a priest. I was smart; smarter than anyone in school, even smarter than the teachers at Manhattan College. Everything came so easy. All marveled at my academic prowess; my logic and, most of all, my focus. I was destined to be great, they said; and I was full of idealism and love for the poor. I thought I could change the world and make it a better place. I saw God in every one I met; or so I thought.

All these years later, I am now 65 years old, living in the splendor of the Cardinal's residence, off Park Avenue in New York; widely admired and acclaimed for my piety and practical stewardship. I have my assistants and my cooks and my helpers waiting on me, ready to meet my whims. They address me, as is customary, as Your Eminence. And I hate that; what a haughty, effected title. I must often meet with the moneyed and elite lay people of the Church; who always seem to be trying to curry favor with me. They are, for the most part; frivolous and phony; out of touch with the struggles of their brethren. They have their charitable causes, but there is no real charity in it. It is just a series of parties amongst their own that masquerade as fundraisers, more social event than anything having to do with charity. There is never any real connection with the people on the street, on the receiving end of their money.

More and more I feel like a commodity, not a person; a prop in some elaborate production outside my control. My interactions with these people are odd and disjointed. It all seems so contrived and unnatural, like a kind of game to see who can get closest to his Eminence; just another status symbol for the rich and privileged supporters. I long for my early days as a parish priest; when I looked in people's eyes, touching their hearts, minds and souls, talking about their problems, making a difference in their lives.

Today has been the worst. I met with seven different people. No sooner had I cajoled a donation of a few thousand dollars from one; I was to meet another patron. I spent hour after hour with these rich benefactors of the church; "putting the arm on them" as I often put it. For maximum results, I manipulate them however I feel I can best extract the most money. Each person has a different motivation in giving; a different button for me to push. Most feel a little guilty; they are usually the old money folks who inherit their fortunes. They are also the most clueless about the stress real people feel; the stress of fearing about your job; the stress about not having a job at all; the stress about having no money to pay a medical bill to take care of your kid or your elderly parent. In a way I feel a little sorry for those folks; so coddled, so naïve, so bland and shallow.

Others, the self made moneyed, are competitive about their gifts; they have to give more than their rivals in business so they can feel superior. They are the narcissists; everything in their life is about their own ego fulfillment. I can size up these Napoleonic princes almost immediately and know exactly how to maneuver them for maximum results. These types smell of cigar smoke and corruption. Maybe they think smoking cigars will bring riches like it did for that old cigar chomper himself, J.P. Morgan. Oftentimes I will just sit silently, after they have filled the room with smoke and bluster about their accomplishments, and watch them squirm. If there is one thing they hate it is absolute silence. They are so insecure that a period of silence longer than five seconds makes them feel awkward and uncomfortable. After about twenty seconds staring at them silently, I will tell them an anonymous donor gave some large sum of money. Their common sense usually capitulates to their ego and tops the sum I named. It's rather humorous. I can just imagine them cursing me out after they have left my presence!

However, on rare occasions, I encounter someone that is actually concerned with the work of the Church; someone who asks questions about programs and makes intelligent observations; someone who is genuine. I can be frank with those people, those rare gems, about where the needs are. I never have to make a suggestion of what I want them to give. These types give from their hearts. I don't have to manipulate them; they actually care. At this point, they care more than I do.

As I sit in my office, I am thankful I have only one more visitor to see today. I look down at my appointment schedule. The last visitor is someone named Arthur Small. I have never met him; his family made some money in textiles or something, and he is a friend of one of the few entertaining donors, the former heavyweight boxing champion Gene Tunney. Maybe Small would be one of those genuine, down-to-earth types. I am hopeful.

As I sit, staring blankly forward, conflicted in thought, a tall handsome man enters the large room. He is dressed in a gray flannel suit with a white shirt and a red and gold tie, stylish but not ostentatious. He looks to be in his early forties. He looks at me in a fast glance and then quickly fixes his eyes to the floor. He speaks.

"Your Eminence, I am Art Small."

I went to shake his hand. Small bowed, bent at the waist, still looking at the floor. From that quick introduction, I can tell that he is not one of those puffed-up old money types. He does not carry himself with that air of superiority. Yet he is different from the new money folks too. His voice is confident, yet he is seemingly humble at the same time. He appears a little self conscious, though, like he is carrying a burden of some kind.

Small continues, "I must apologize up front. I do not have much time tonight. Weeks ago, I promised to get back to 34th Street to help with dinner tonight at the soup kitchen. One thing I do; I never breaks promises; not to anyone, especially not to my employees or the volunteers on 34th Street. So let's keep the small talk to a minimum. Let's get right into what I can do for the Church and I will not take up much of your time; I know you are busy. I've been blessed with some financial resources and we're in this damn depression. I need to share some of my good fortune with some who have less. I started the soup kitchen on 34th Street near my plant with that in mind; but I can do some more for you."

I am immediately impressed; a man who gets right to the point. I have heard of the 34th Street soup kitchen. Tunney had told him about all the "poor bastards on 34th Street"; the homeless, the unemployed, the drunks and the other misbegotten, who were fed there every day.

"Art," I asked, "How often do you work down in the kitchen serving food?"

"Not nearly enough actually," Small answered. "I run the financial side of it in my spare time. But I have to run my business and spend time with my wife and kids too. But I try for at least twice a month actually serving the patrons. I look in the eyes of those poor people and it humbles me; you know, it gives me perspective on my own life. I usually take my eight year old kid with me. He needs to learn to not take our money for granted; that our money is a resource to be stewarded, not squandered. I promised to take him tonight; so I gotta leave soon. So let's get down to brass tacks, I can probably afford to donate about $400,000 to your causes. I need the rest of my surplus to keep the kitchen going."

I meekly hang my head. I miss the service to the poor that I experienced as a parish priest. Now my life has become a series of ceremonies, engulfed in splendor, with no heart and no soul. This man Art seems to be touching people, the way I used to. Art seems full of fervor, full of passion and full of life. Energy emanates from the very being of Art Small. I look at Art for a long while and say nothing. I should feel envy, but I am beyond that now. I feel nothing. My life is now so empty.

"What's wrong, your Eminence? You look tired. You're sitting there like you saw a ghost or something. I am sorry if you expected more money; but that is all I can do, honest. I am being earnest."

"It's not the money, Art. I appreciate your generosity. I am just tired; really, really tired."

We sat across from each other for what seemed like a minute. Yet the pause is not planned or purposely uncomfortable like the planned silences I thrust onto the J.P Morgan types. Art is a thoughtful man, not apt to talk just to fill the air with words. Small looked at my face all the while, studied it, as if he was trying to read my thoughts. He seemed to understand.

"May I suggest a vacation for his Eminence? I'll give you the keys to my beach house. It's a nice big house on the top of a bluff; with a beautiful beach at its feet. It is September now, so you won't be bothered with crowds; you will have time to think and reflect. I go there whenever I feel blue; to rejuvenate. After a week there, you will have all your energy back, I promise. Here are the keys. Give me a piece of paper; I'll write down the address. Call me when you get back. I have to go now. Good bye."

And with that, Art Small left the office, leaving me to contemplate my next move. I looked on the piece of paper that Mr. Small left on my desk. It read as follows: "50 Bluff Avenue, Watch Hill, Rhode Island-fishing poles are in the back shed". I didn't know what to make of it.

The offer came quickly; it was odd and generous, but most impressively it was sincere and heartfelt. Small didn't seem to be looking for any favors either. His eyes told me of his concern for me; not as the Cardinal, but as another human being. It seemed simply a kind gesture from an ostensible stranger; there were no strings attached.

I have not taken a vacation in years. I always thought I didn't need them. But right now, at this moment, I need something, anything, to shake myself from these doldrums; to wake myself from this melancholy. I am drowning; maybe Small is tossing me a life preserver. Something is telling me to go. If I can capture some of the energy that Small seemed to have in his bottle, maybe a trip would be good. My calendar is light, the schools are all open and I already raised enough money today to feed the Church's ravenous appetite for a long while. The decision is final. I will inform the staff and take off in my new car, a 1932 Ford Model A, in the morning.

I awaken at 5:00 a.m. the next morning, early as is my custom. I inform my staff that I will be away for a few days to attend to some family business and that I will be back for next Sunday Mass at St.

Patrick's Cathedral. I had pulled out a map the night before and was all set with the directions of how to get to the beach house. It was Tuesday September 11, 1934, and I, Patrick Cardinal Hayes, would begin my first vacation in many, many years. I started off at about 9:00 a.m. I estimated that the trip would take about six or seven hours; up through the Bronx and continuing North on Route 1 through Connecticut until I reached the Rhode Island border. The town of Watch Hill was about a mile and a half south of Route 1, right on the water, the most Southwestern point in the small state. I had never been up there before.

The ride up the coast is tranquil and relaxing. It is just me, my car, the warm sunshine and the cooling breeze blowing through the windows. Because I do not want any undue attention, I wear my priest's collar without any of the Cardinal's vestments. The Big City seems a world away as I meander through the small coastal towns in Connecticut. The bright autumn sun illuminates the villages I ride through, each one distinct and beautiful in its own way. Fishing villages, farming communities, lush green pastures and even small cities all seem to whisper soothingly to me, telling me to unwind. And even though I preach weekly in one of the most ornate cathedrals in the entire World,

I marvel at the loveliness of the small white churches that blend modestly and harmoniously into the New England landscape.

At around 3:30 that afternoon, I veer off of Route 1 towards Watch Hill. The car hugs the road along the east bank of the Pawcatuck River which acts as the natural border between the states of Rhode Island and Connecticut. After a few minutes I reach the crest of the hill which overlooks my destination. As I slow down at the hilltop to survey the setting of my retreat, I am greeted by a cool sea breeze which smells of bayberry. I am pleased; it is idyllic and inviting. I slowly drive my car down Bay Street, the main drag in town; which is filled with many quaint shops. In front of me, to my right, a spit of land forms a peninsula which provides a natural harbor on one side and a long sandy beach on the other. At the end of the street sits a small restaurant and a little carousal with elegantly painted wooden horses.

The road takes a sharp bend to the left and leads up Bluff Avenue. As I ride up the hill I am greeted by large Victorian homes with vast green lawns that roll fluently toward the ocean. An outsized yellow Hotel sits atop the hill. A tall white lighthouse stands majestically amid the grandeur of the large homes on a little piece of land that juts out arrogantly into the ocean. The lighthouse stands prominent and sturdy like a big brother, protecting the village against any fury the sea might proffer. At the bottom of the bluff is another long stretch of sandy beach. Within a minute, I spot my accommodations and drive into the driveway at 50 Bluff Avenue.

The view from atop the bluff is inspiring. The sun shines warmly and brightly on the ocean and sand sitting at the bottom of the hill. The house is a large white clapboard structure with a crows nest atop the third floor. It is stately and grandiose, much more lavish than I would have expected on my trip up. Nevertheless, as I enter the house I am filled with serenity rather than awe at its majesty. There is nothing like the splendor of nature to restore ones faith. I open the windows and a warm steady breeze blows from the ocean through the house; seemingly saying welcome, take rest. I am a little tired from the drive, so I walk up to the second floor and pick a bedroom to take a nap.

I am awakened what seems shortly after I start my nap, but it is now dark; my bedroom illuminated only by the bright full moon that now shines off the ocean and the occasional flash of light from the lighthouse, which moves in a semicircle throwing a stream of light towards the water. I am now wide awake and it is about two o'clock in the morning based on my estimate of where the moon hangs in the sky. Maybe if I take a stroll I will be able to go back to sleep. So I put on a sweater over my head and walk down a gravel road to the lighthouse. At the end of the road is the lighthouse, which is immediately surrounded by a plush lawn, which is, in turn, surrounded on three sides by an elaborate sea wall; a network of large granite stones used to protect the lighthouse from the ocean.

As I walk along the rocks, I notice a man about my age sitting comfortably among them, fishing. He speaks, "Good evening. Can't sleep?"

"No," I answer. "I fell asleep early this afternoon and just got up. I'm visiting your lovely hamlet from New York."

"Have a seat. It's a beautiful night. An easy one for me; this moon is so bright tonight, we probably don't even need to shine the light. On nights like these I just do a little fishing, do a little thinking and check on the light every few hours. I'm Larry Congdon, the keeper of the light here in Watch Hill."

"Pat Hayes, glad to meet you," I say as I shake his hand. "Those rocks look comfortable; do you mind if I take a seat?"

"Nope; by all means, sit," he answers.

As we sit side by side, the waves lap lazily against the rocks. Larry tells me some history of the lighthouse. There were some hairy moments. In 1872, the steamer Metis collided with a schooner about a mile out. Jared Crandall, the keeper at the time, getting help from some others, managed to save 33 people, although about 130 souls perished. And in February 1907, the Larchmont went down in the middle of a blizzard; and about 200 lost their lives in that disaster. There are some shoals southwest of here that can be troublesome on occasion. There had been a few other minor maritime disasters over the years as a result of those shoals, but Larry did his best to try and avert problems and fix things.

"But you can't always stop bad things from happening," Larry opined. "Sometimes the Lord whips up the Ocean with such powerful wind, rain and snow that you just feel so small. I can't tell you why he lets it happen, but I guess he has his reasons. In those times he tries me; he tests my will. Most of the time it is quiet and peaceful here; but you have to be ready, you have to be vigilant. You never know when it will be your time. The test of a man is not when things are good but when things get complicated and difficult; when it seems you have so many things to fix, you don't know exactly what to fix first. You know, I think God is testing our whole country right now with this depression. But we'll be okay. This fellow Roosevelt seems to know how to get through hard times; he tries to fix things, but he don't panic. When the storm hits, you have to hop into action and still keep your head. Never panic, just do your best; things will work out. That's what a keeper of the light has to do."

I asked, "Did you ever pull anyone out of the water, save their life? That would be gratifying."

"You see that rowboat over there? I have used that little boat many times to pull people out of the waves. It is very crowded here in the summer and sometimes the waves can get rough. I keep my eyes and ears open. When you pull someone out of the water, they have a lot of gratitude. Their eyes speak their appreciation. A scare in the waves like that might actually be good for someone, though, it lets them know they are mortal; no better or worse than anyone else. I remember pulling one kid out of the water many years ago, Art Small was his name. He was a rich arrogant, wise guy teenager; real cocky. When I pulled him out of those waves, I looked in his eyes and I knew he had changed. Something came over him, like an epiphany. From that moment on, he became the best kid going. Now he's grown up. He brings his own kids here in the summer; a wonderful guy."

Larry continued. "As gratifying as it is to feel that thank you from one individual you pull out of the water; that isn't the most important thing you do as a lighthouse keeper. It's just keeping that light on every night, shining so all can see, that is what's really important. By shining that light you never know how many lives you save. If that ship carrying 600 souls averts that shoal because I kept the light going; well then I saved 600 souls and never even knew about it. How many lives have I helped save just by keeping that light on night after night? I'll never know. And I'll never get a thank you for it, but that is the truly important work."

I listened and talked a lot to my new friend tonight. Soon the sun was beginning to rise in back of us. So I bade farewell. And as much as I am enjoying the breathtaking surroundings, surely a gift from God, I now know I have to get back soon to my own lighthouse in New York City; St. Patrick's Cathedral. So I can shine a beacon down on the congregation and the tourists and maybe save a soul or 600, just like Larry does every night.

When I returned to St. Patrick's the next Sunday and gave my sermon; a parable about a lighthouse keeper named Larry, I knew that I, along with every other member of humanity to a varying degree, am a keeper of the light. As I gazed out on the pews filled with people, my eyes locked briefly with the eyes of Art Small. He nodded approvingly and smiled. He understood. And now so did I.

The Diary of Angela Conley

The Diary of Angela Conley is about a thirteen year old girl and her unique relationship with her 103 year old great-grandfather.

The Diary of Angela Conley

January 29, 2005

It is Saturday January 29, 2005, my thirteenth birthday. I eat my cereal, turn on the television and there he is; the overweight balding weatherman who wears the bow tie, announcing the birthdays of those few folks who hit the century mark of over 100 birthdays, today. It's amazing that in a country of 300 million people, only a handful hit triple figures each day and my Poppa is one of them. I'm going to have some friends from school over to our house to celebrate my birthday tonight. But before that can happen, I have to go visit my great-grandfather Angelo Petrelli, the man I call Poppa, down at the nursing home in Coney Island. I was named Angela after him because, like him, I was born on January 29th. That's right, Poppa is exactly 90 years older than me; he turns 103 today. From his 100th birthday, we have had a little tradition; we celebrate our birthday together with a visit and three cupcakes, one for him, one for Mom and one for me.

Mom and I get in the car for the ride down to Brooklyn from our home in Westchester County, just outside of New York City. Since Mom has taken to deem all the rap music on the radio as vulgar, I am trapped having to either amuse myself by looking at the scenery of the Bronx or by playing Super Mario Brothers for the thirty-eight thousandth time. I opt to note the scenery and listen grudgingly to her Paul Simon music. As we drive down the New York State Thruway in the Bronx, past Yankee Stadium, a little apartment building right next to the highway catches my eye because it has a lighthouse on its roof; pretty neat I think, never saw that before. In Upper Manhattan, we go by a handball court with primitive, yet intricate, painting on its wall and the saying "Crack is Wack". It's a Keith Haring original painting in a random, obscure outdoor location in Harlem; art for the masses, thank you Keith. We continue past the Brooklyn Bridge, down past South Street Seaport and Wall Street and head to the Brooklyn Battery Tunnel, under the water. I never thought about it before, but this is actually pretty amazing what we are doing; going under the water with all these other cars, starting out in Manhattan and ending up in Brooklyn. How did they build this and keep the water out? I ask Mom and she doesn't know. I suppose I'll just have to read about it myself if I get the chance; and I probably won't get the chance with all the darn homework I get now.

We drive several more minutes through the grayness that is Brooklyn, until we arrive at the Seacrest Nursing Home on 24th Street in Coney Island; right down the street from the beach and Boardwalk. The sun peeks through the clouds and I am surprised to see a high level of activity on the sand in the middle of winter; joggers, walkers, a group of kids playing football and two guys in their bathrobes wearing bathing suits. Mom says those two guys in their bathrobes are part of the Polar Bear Club, a group that swims in the frigid ocean all winter. I am not so sure; they look more like they could be psychotic flashers to me. The legendary Coney Island roller coaster and amusement park hover near us dormant, hibernating for the winter. The neighborhood is a little run-down my mother comments, not as nice as it used to be, but I don't really notice that. The sea air is crisp; fresher and friendlier than the air is at home. That is why Poppa wanted to be in this place, so he could be near his memories of frolicking in the ocean here; so he could see and smell his youth.

As we enter his room on the fourth floor, my mother greets him. "Hey Poppa, it's Nancy and Angela; Happy Birthday."

"What day is it? It's January 29th again? It seems like every year it's January 29th at least once. Angela do you know what happened 85 years ago today?"

"Poppa, it's your birthday, you are 103. You were born 103 years ago, not 85 years ago," I remind him.

"I know that, but I arrived in this country on my 18th birthday; January 29, 1920. I never told you that? On my birthday; on our birthday. Happy Birthday Angela. Well anyways, are you being a good kid; listening to your mom?"

"Sure." I answer.

"What are you studying in school these days, kid?"

"Well, we're doing a unit on immigration. I have to write a short narrative pretending to be an immigrant. I plan on writing what it was like to be an Italian immigrant at the beginning of last century."

"Angela, do you need some sources for that?" my Mom interjects, "I know someone with some first-hand experience as an Italian immigrant at the beginning of the last century and he is sitting right in front of me."

Wow, she's right; quite a rarity that is. I never thought about using Poppa as a source, but that might work out great. I'm here; he's here and the assignment is due in a few weeks. I could interview him and get some good stuff; maybe cut down on the research a little bit with some anecdotal material. "If it's okay with you Poppa, would you share some of your experiences with me?"

"Anything to help," he answers. "But can I have my cupcake first? I'm a little hungry."

When Mom pulls out the cupcakes, Poppa grabs one and starts munching.

In a soft gravelly voice he launches into his soliloquy, "Well, the world was very different when I came over from Italy. World War I had just ended in 1918 and many of my friends were slaughtered in the fighting. I was from Southern Italy; Sicily, an island off the Mainland and I fought in The Great War with many of the young guys from my village, including my closest friend at the time, Vito Luciano. Coincidentally, Vito was born on the same day as both of us, Angela; January 29. Anyways, you know that saying, war is hell? It's true. Hell is being in the mountains in the snow, wind and cold; sick, hungry and exhausted, waiting and waiting for your turn to get your head shot off. We fought battle after battle in the cold of the Southern Alps; and General Cadorna was nuts. He kept sending us right at the Austrians who were perched up in the hills; we were sitting ducks. It was pretty in the summer with the lakes and snow-capped mountains all around, but you couldn't really enjoy the scenery; you were too busy paying attention to just staying alive. Well one day in July 1918 Vito got hit in his arm, just below the shoulder as we retreated from one of our assaults on the

119

Austrians. When I saw my friend lying there, I quickly threw off my gear and ripped off a piece of cloth to use as a bandage. I threw Vito over my shoulder and carried him. Lieutenant DeMatteo said to leave him to die; but at that point, after almost three years of obeying orders, I couldn't obey any more. I cared more about my friend Vito than about the damn chain of command. So as the troops moved forward, I trudged Vito along over my shoulder, descending the hills, through the shallow Piave River. The sounds of war were all around us. I heard bullets whiz by, hitting trees and splashing into the water. But Vito and I were lucky that day; God was with us, I guess. I found our troop about two miles from where Vito was shot and they patched him up good so he could fight some more. We weren't sure why we were fighting, we were just fighting. And in the fall they told us to stop fighting, the war was over; so we stopped.

Vito and I went back to Sicily, but things weren't the same as before. The Spanish flu was everywhere. People were dying all around us; just like in the war. First they would get the flu and then pneumonia and then they would quietly pass on; it was awful. And the doctors had no cure for the flu or the pneumonia; penicillin was not around yet. You don't understand about that, Angela, but you could die from the flu back then! A lot of our friends had died in the War and all the ones who didn't die were either hanging around drinking too much or headed to America. By the end of 1919, there was nothing left for me on Sicily; my parents died of the flu within two months of each other, early in the year. I could do stone work for construction; but there was no work, no one had any money and the government was inept as to how to make things better. Everyone was gloomy; hope was gone, completely drained from the Italian spirit. The proud country that produced the Roman Empire, Leonardo DaVinci and Michelangelo was brought to its knees by a war, a contagion and some selfish, corrupt politicos. So at the end of 1919, Vito and I decided to get the hell out and head to America. You might think we would be scared; young, heading halfway across the world and not knowing any English. But we were eager and excited; after all, the legend was that the streets were paved in gold. And most of all we were just plain sick of where things seemed to be heading in Sicily. So we cleaned the slate, took all our money and boarded a boat for New York City.

We were lucky in a way that life in Sicily had become so glum, so quickly. It forced us to move to America if we wanted a better life. I came through Ellis Island in 1920, when there were no limits to the number of Italians who could enter the country. The only limits were public health concerns, and I was healthy and strong. In 1921, just one year after I got here, President Harding signed the Quota Act. That Act put limits on the number of immigrants who could come into America. You know what I learned from that? Be decisive; don't ever hesitate or second guess yourself if you think you are right. Make a decision and go with it, for better or worse. If I had languished in Sicily, wavering about whether or not to go to America, I may have had my entrance here postponed indefinitely because of the quotas.

The boat ride from Italy was filthy; we were in third class, the worst accommodations on the ship. It was damp and putrid smelling, and there were rats and insects all around us. The food was not fit for a dog and a lot of the other passengers were complaining and whining. But having been through the War, it was a piece of cake for Vito and me. We helped some of the deckhands do some of their chores in exchange for a few lessons in the English language. We practiced our English together as best we could so that by the time we entered New York Harbor, we would both be proficient enough in English so no one could give us a hard time. The arrival in New York was widely anticipated and once we reached New York Harbor, it was unmistakable. When we caught glimpse of the Statue of Liberty, our hearts pounded and the boat erupted in applause.

In a few short minutes the boat was tied up at Ellis Island, where the officials sized you up to see if you were to be allowed into America. When we offloaded at Ellis Island, Vito and I were processed quickly. The English we learned along the way came in handy. The immigration officials asked us what we did for a living and I said I was a stone mason; Vito said he was a fisherman. They asked us why we were here and we both said we were war vets and wanted to start anew, that we were sick of Italy. Apparently that was what they wanted to hear, so they let us through quickly. The folks who spoke no English had a much more difficult time and were told to stand in a second long line. We didn't stick around Ellis Island for long once we were processed; we caught the first available ferry to Manhattan.

Once we hit Manhattan, we got off of the ferry and a curious thing happened. A man called to us in Italian and asked our names and where we were from.

"Angelo Petrelli from Palermo in Sicily," I answered. "I am looking for work and a place to sleep. I am a stone mason but am honest, strong and willing to work hard. Perhaps you could direct me to a local church where they speak Italian. I am sure they will help me there." I was wary of this guy, he wore a suit and tie, he seemed a little too slick to me, like some of the wise guys I avoided back in Palermo.

"I am Vito Luciano, also from Palermo, and I am looking for the streets paved in gold," Vito said laughing.

The man looked slightly surprised; then with a grin asked, "Are you related to Salvatore Luciano?"

"I have a cousin who came over to America with his parents years ago by that name, but we haven't heard from him in years. Why do you ask?"

"Come with me, friend. I know your cousin. I'll bring you to him; perhaps he will want to give you some work. As for you Mr. Petrelli, I will show you to the Catholic Church you seek; Most Precious Blood Church on Mulberry Street. Come on guys."

We jumped into the man's automobile and I was dropped off at the Church on Mulberry Street; Vito and Slick drove off in the automobile to meet Vito's cousin. It seems Vito's cousin was a fellow named Salvatore "Lucky" Luciano and he ran the rackets in New York. My poor friend Vito got sucked into the life of a gangster, right off the boat, courtesy of his good, caring cousin Salvatore. And as many came to know, once Lucky Luciano got his hooks into you, it was impossible to get away from him.

After getting out of the car, I stopped into the church and noted that the steps were falling apart. I located the parish priest, Father Pasquale, and said to him in Italian that I would patch up the steps, no charge, if he could direct me to a place to stay for the night. He said I could sleep on the floor in the rectory for one night and that there was cement and tools in the basement that I could use for the job. So I patched up the steps for Father Pat that day. When I was done, I showed him my work and he was pleased. I slept on the floor in the rectory my first night in America with a donated blanket that Father Pat said I could keep. The floor was wood, so it wasn't so cold, and in good shape except for one floor board that was loose. I slept well my first night in America and the next morning I was awakened by the Father and a parishioner named Mr. Aiello who wanted some work done at his apartment building. Apparently Father Pat recommended me to Mr. Aiello after examining my work on the church steps.

So I went to the apartment building and inspected it. It was in pretty bad shape; so I started immediately and worked into the darkness to get everything done that was necessary. And when Mr. Aiello examined my work, he too was pleased, just like Father Pat had been. He said his building superintendent had just left and asked if I would like to assume the position as his new superintendent. I accepted on the spot. The job pay was for $35.00 a week and a free apartment in the basement.

And it was good work because I could fit in side jobs that people wanted done to make money on the side. My reputation spread as I did more and more jobs in the neighborhood. My work was neat and I worked fast; I had a steady stream of side jobs and was getting lots of repeat business. Pretty soon I had enough money to open a bank account at the local bank that catered to the Italian immigrants and each week I would put a few dollars in it. And even though I only had a small sullied room next to the coal furnace in the basement, with only a sink and a toilet, I was happy. There was work and hope and optimism, things that were in low supply back in Sicily.

And living in Little Italy made the transition to America easier. I learned English at my own pace and read the Italian newspaper to keep up with what was going on. I had lots of friends and acquaintances in the neighborhood with the same interests. I liked America, even though my living conditions in Italy were a little nicer.

Two years later, my life changed completely. I remember it like yesterday. I went to Mass one Sunday morning and when I was leaving, my eyes locked on your great-grandmother Marie. She had dark hair and beautiful big black eyes. Her olive skin gave her away as a Sicilian, just like me. I said hello and instantly we clicked. We wanted to spend all our time together from that moment on. And after a courtship of about a year, we were married. I convinced Mr. Aiello to give me a nicer apartment upstairs and agreed to start paying him rent. After our wedding in the afternoon, we celebrated our honeymoon; a Saturday night on Mulberry Street, painting the walls of our new apartment and sharing a meal of Pasta Primavera, red wine, salad and garlic bread. I thought I died and went to heaven.

We immediately started to grow our family and after five years we had three children; Tony, Vinnie and your grandmother Levia. It was pretty crowded with five of us in a one bedroom apartment; but we were comfortable and happy. I had become friends with a guy in the neighborhood called Tony Ice who moved out to Brooklyn shortly after I was married. He had a truck and I helped him deliver coal and ice when I wasn't doing my stonework or fulfilling my duties as Super.

Angela, you might find this interesting, we didn't have freezers or refrigerators; we had iceboxes. Refrigerators and freezers didn't come to the masses until the middle of the 1930's. Before that, you dropped a big block of ice in the icebox and stored your food in it. If the ice melted, your food spoiled, so people really needed ice deliveries back then. And I made great side money helping Tony deliver ice and coal.

Tony had a business philosophy that went something like this. Don't sell people what they want, sell them what they need. Wants can change like the weather, but needs are always. There are three things people always need: food, clothes and shelter. The ice kept the food fresh and the coal kept the folks warm; they needed these things. In the depression, people only had money for things they needed. So guys like Tony and I always had work, even though there were so many other folks out of work during the depression.

We used to go out to Coney Island on the subway and meet up with Tony's family. Coney Island in those days was the only place you could go to get away. Only rich folks could afford a vacation; but it didn't matter to us. A daytrip to Coney Island was better than any vacation those rich folks could have dreamed up. The beach was wide and sandy, the water was clean and clear, and the Boardwalk and amusements were like nothing in the world as far as we were concerned. And everyone was friendly. There were no drugs, no gangs and none of the garbage that goes on today. Tony eventually bought a three-family house in Brooklyn and we moved in there upstairs from him, his first tenants. And Marie and I had a great life with your grandmother and her brothers.

The kids all turned out great. You know all about your grandma; but your grand-uncles were terrific too. Both fought bravely in World War II; Tony in Europe and Vinnie in the Pacific. And your grand-uncles both also worked on the Brooklyn Battery Tunnel, the Verrazano Bridge and a host of other roads and bridge projects all around New York. I have to say moving to America was a struggle, but it was the best struggle I could have ever bargained for myself. And as I look back, I am thankful for all my struggles and hard work. As odd as this may sound to a thirteen year old kid, I think that a life without struggle is not even worth living. If things come too easy, you don't appreciate them."

As he said this, the alarm in my head went off. He's preaching, he's preaching; time to change the subject, time to change the subject. I cut him off at the pass. "So whatever happened to your friend Vito?" I asked.

"Funny you should ask that Angela. You'll never believe this one. In the winter of 1946, I got a visit from Vito. It was the last time I ever saw him. I made him some coffee, pulled out some biscotti, and we talked. He said he was having some problems with the authorities. He acknowledged that the business he was in was highly profitable, but risky and dangerous. And he couldn't live too lavishly because the Internal Revenue Service had its eye trained on him; they were trying to nail him on tax evasion charges. Recalling that afternoon in the Alps all those years ago, he recognized that he owed his life to me. He said he understood me and trusted me, that I was honest beyond reproach. He also said he respected me for not getting mixed up in his gangster shenanigans and for living straight-up. He hated that life, always looking over his shoulder wondering who would double-cross him or even outright kill him. That life had destroyed his marriage and he was

131

disappointed that he had just his one son. He envied the family life that Marie and I had.

But Vito was into the life too deep; he couldn't get out and he needed a favor, fast. The heat from the IRS was ceaseless and Vito needed to hide some of his assets. In his arms Vito cradled a large wooden box with a three number lock built into it. He instructed me to hold it for him until he needed it. He didn't want its existence known to anyone, just me. Hold onto it until I come back for it, he told me, I'll make sure no wise-guys ever give you any grief. I told him I didn't want to hold it, but he ignored me. He just got up and left the box right there on the table, disappearing quickly down the street in a large Lincoln.

This stinks, I thought. I don't know what is in this box, but knowing Vito it could be anything. And I didn't want it in my home. So I took it and went down to the Church. I thought of a safe place to put it, recalling my first night in America when I slept on the creaky floor in the rectory. I looked at the floor where I had slept, remembering the loose floorboard underneath me. A rug now covered the spot. After moving the rug, I noticed the floorboard was still loose and so were several of the planks right next to it too. That's probably why Father had the rug there; to cover the loose planks. So I tracked down Father Rotundi and said I noticed his floor needed fixing. I asked if I could fix it for him; I could get it done in one afternoon. He was agreeable to that, I had done so much other work at the Church gratis and he said he expected this work to also be gratis. I said that would be no problem, I would even put it in writing, and Father Rotundi smiled, thinking he got one over on me. So I drafted an agreement saying I would fix the floor for free whenever I determined it to be in disrepair, as long as I am alive. Father Rotundi and I quickly signed it and I commenced the work. I ripped out the old floor boards, placed the box below the floor in the crawl space and fixed the floor, good as new.

Fast forward about forty years, somewhere around 1988, when Reagan was President, I got word that Vito had died at the age of 86; such a young man. They said it was an accident, but I'm not so sure. People in Vito's line of work seemed a lot more prone to dying of accidents than the rest of us. Anyways, by then that old box had been sitting there for forty years and with old Vito passed on, there was no chance he would be asking for it back anytime soon. So I went down to the

Church, looked at the floor and informed old Monsignor Rotundi that it was time for me to do a little upkeep on the floor again. And per our agreement, it would be free of charge. I got the green light from Monsignor shortly thereafter and I replaced the floor again, this time removing the box from underneath. And guess what, I still have that box, it is in my closet over there. There is only one problem with it, I don't know the combination."

How cool, I thought. Let's take a look at it. Quickly I popped up from my seat and grabbed the box sitting on the floor in Poppa's closet. I brought it over to his bed and said, "Let me try 1-2-9, the numbers of our birthday, Poppa."

And when I punched in those numbers, don't you know, that lid popped right open, revealing piles of wrapped money, stacked in neat orderly piles; more money than I had ever seen.

Poppa observed, "That's more money than I have ever seen." It looked like all fifty and hundred dollar bills too. "Let's count it," I implored. And so we did.

134

It took about ten minutes for the three of us to count the money; we counted slowly and carefully. Each group of twenty bills was wrapped in a rubber band. There were twenty groups of fifty dollar bills and twenty groups of one hundred dollar bills; $60,000 in all. And on the bottom of the box was an envelope addressed to Angelo Petrelli. Poppa asked that I read it to him since his 103 year old eyes were failing a bit. I obliged. The letter read as follows:

1/29/46

Dear Angelo,

I've made a lot of mistakes in life and now I am paying for them; it is stressful always having to watch my back. But I have no regrets. I chose this life and that is how it is; I can't undo my mistakes. As to you, I will always feel closer to you than to anyone. We grew up together, we went to war together, and we came to America together. And you risked your life to save mine up in those hills in Northern Italy. I can never repay you for that. But, if I die before you, keep this money as a small thank you for saving my life back then. And remember, when you play the numbers, 1-2-9 is always a good bet.

Your Fratello,

Vito Luciano

"Poppa, what's a fratello?" I asked.

"Fratello is Italian for brother. But to an Italian, it's much more than that. A fratello is someone who you deeply care for and honor. You know what I learned in this country; anyone can be your fratello, not just an Italian. You should always take care of your brothers."

"Poppa, we have to go," my Mom said. "Let me lock up that money and put it back in your closet."

"No Nancy, you take it. I don't need anything and I lived without it this long. I know someone who I believe needs it more than me; to go to college, my sorellina, Angela. Use it for her."

"Poppa, what's a sorellina?"

"It means little sister. You are my little sister, Angela; born on the same day and named after me. One last piece of advice before you go; use your time wisely. Always bear in mind that folks like me and you only get around 103 years," he said smiling. "And remember, even after I'm gone, I'll be watching over you. Have a great birthday with your friends. Go. Get out of here."

And so, after hugging Poppa, we left. I, a thirteen year old girl, and Mom, all five feet one of her, and a box filled with $60,000 in cash, walking unguarded in the mean streets of Coney Island. Luckily nobody smelled the money along the way as we walked to the car without incident and drove off.

While driving home, I asked, "Mom, how many great-grandchildren does Poppa have?"

"Well, you, your sister Jillian and both Uncle Vinnie and Uncle Tony have two grandchildren each. So he has six in total."

"So why did he give all the money to me? Shouldn't each of the six get some?"

"Yes, Angela, I guess I agree. That would only be fair. When we get home, I'll call my cousins and let them know what happened. And each of you great-grandchildren will get a $10,000 share of the loot."

And I thought to myself, Vito, wherever you are, in heaven or in hell, thanks fratello. And I smiled broadly. I had a party back home to get to and a lot of friends to celebrate with.

Jillian's Grandpa

Jillian's Grandpa is about the genius of innocence and its place in the circle of life.

Jillian's Grandpa

If you stand on the docks of the old Brooklyn Navy Yard today it's empty and cold. The docks are aged and rotting, pretty much deserted, and the winter wind whips ceaselessly off the water and cuts through you like a dagger. The land sits solitary and vacant, like an urban ghost town in the middle of the busiest city in the world. But if you look across the water, the thing you cannot miss is the view; the unobstructed panorama of the Manhattan skyline along with the magnificent grandeur of the Statue of Liberty. That's what the modern real estate developers see too, as they stand on these old decaying piers and hatch their development schemes; as they try to reinvent this gritty old shipyard as something new and glitzy. They see the glamorous skyline across the water, so close you could almost touch it; they see the potential for luxury apartments, for shopping, for office buildings, for a movie studio, even for a new sports arena. But for old-timers like Jillian's grandfather, these new plans for development are bittersweet. Sure, development would revitalize the area and restore glamour once again to this decaying part of Brooklyn. But it is also a tad sad to imagine the place where he worked all those years, so hard and so long, changing into something so different. The thought of the Navy Yard as a playpen for the well-heeled was as incongruous to him as Clint Eastwood eating sushi. It didn't look right and it didn't smell right.

Jillian's grandfather Paul was a robust man, short but powerful; with arms made hard and muscled from over forty years working on these docks in the Red Hook Section of Brooklyn and from pumping iron at the local gym. He toiled all those years and saw ships come in from all over the world; enormous, spectacular vessels that served every function you could imagine: military ships, cruise ships, commercial ships and even aircraft carriers. He saw the boom times in the 1940's and 1950's, when over 20,000 people worked for his employer, Todd Shipyards; and he saw the down times when the operations were shut down entirely, right after he retired, one of only a handful of men remaining from the glory years.

It had been a good run; no, a great run. He started in the shipyards in 1929, right before the Great Depression; a 13 year old kid who lied about his age and said he was 16. He had no discernable skills save his strength, his Brooklyn street-smarts and his ability to work long and hard. And because of those traits and the fact that he was a quick study with mechanical things, he held that job right on through the Depression until the War started. And in 1941, when he tried to sign up to go to Europe, they told him his hearing wasn't good enough to join the Army. So he stayed in the shipyards through the War years and worked on the military vessels that populated the docks and the yard.

After he retired in 1983, he continued to live where he always had; with his wife in their Brooklyn apartment. He liked it there. It was familiar; it was comfortable. He lived there for forty years and he knew where everything was. He could walk to everything and he knew where to get everything he needed. The best fruit-stand was on 86th Street, the best pastries were on Bay 13th and the best pizza was a place over on Third Avenue where you could smell the garlic a block away. But as he got older, he noticed things didn't seem the same. The neighborhood was changing. The neighborhood was now referred to simply as the "hood", they took the neighbor out of the word. And he thought that idiom change aptly summed up what was happening. With few neighborly characteristics, with rising crime and the various ethnic groups clannishly keeping to themselves, it no longer had the warm feel of community. The old friends seemed to pass on or move away, except for the relatives, the other elderly brothers and sisters of him and his wife. It was his duty to take care of them, to make sure they went to their doctors and got their medication.

He didn't like the neighborhood changes. He held onto the past like a treasure. He longed for the days when people could say America is the greatest nation in the world and still mean it; when that categorization of our nation was a reality and not a cliché that politicians dusted off during elections. As he got older, he seemed to complain even more about where the world was headed. On the surface he was just like any other grumpy old curmudgeon. But if you looked at it a little differently, you realized there was actually a bizarre optimism in his apparent crabbiness. His complaints weren't really complaints at all, but simple yearning for a then that he thought was much better than the now; pure nostalgia for the goodness and happiness that he had lived.

Most people look forward in time to see how to make life better; he just looked backwards for his clues to improvement.

Coney Island and Miami Beach were his magical and special places. He would talk about all the good times; of swimming in the ocean and fishing and running up and down the beach for no other reason than the sheer joy of running up and down the beach for the fun of it. But now Coney Island and Miami Beach aren't the same places; the developers changed all that. They built and built and built until it was so crowded they couldn't build anymore. And all that building didn't make anything better; it just made it more hectic and crowded and chaotic. But Coney Island and Miami Beach would rise again to their former majesty, Grandpa would say; just you watch, the world will come to its senses one of these days.

His daughter had a different view. She went to college, got her MBA and moved out of the hood. Unlike her dad, Nancy didn't foresee a rebound in the cards for the neighborhood. Although she too loved the neighborhood, she was resigned that it had degenerated into simply a "hood". So she looked beyond its boundaries, the modern day version of a pioneer. And that's where Nancy met me, beyond the boundaries of the hood. We got married in the hood, in the same church she always went to, and that made Grandpa Paul happy. A few years later we gave him a present; her name was Jillian.

Jillian was Paul's granddaughter; a little bit of devil and a little bit of angel. She looked a lot like her Grandpa, with her reddish blond hair, her deep blue eyes and her sly smile that made everyone around her happy. Jillian liked to climb all over her Grandpa Paul and he liked to grab her and toss her above his head. Jillian would scream with glee when he would bellow, "Jillian, do you want to fly?" And he would laugh; it seemed like Jillian was the only person who could make him laugh anymore. And because he was so strong he would fling little Jillian a lot higher than he should have. But there was no harm, we knew he would never let her drop and the higher he threw her the more she loved it.

In the old days, he used to be brawny and muscular. He loved to pump iron and his physique reflected that. And even though he wouldn't hurt a fly, no one would ever mess with Grandpa Paul. He used to lift weights in the old days with a neighborhood kid named Lou Ferrigno. Ferrigno went on to win bodybuilding contests all over the World. And although Ferigno was a lot younger than Paul, they had a little kinship going. Ferrigno, like Paul, was hard of hearing; almost deaf. But now, as a retired old man in a changing neighborhood, he was a target, especially around the tenth of the month. That is when the vultures would wait outside the local bank branches for the old-timers to cash their social security checks.

So one day, right around the 10th of April 2000, he was back in Brooklyn, walking his sister-in-law to the eye doctor. A local thug looked at him and his sister-in-law and thought they were simple pickings for some easy cash. So as Paul walked his sister-in-law to her appointment, he felt the presence of someone over his shoulder. The person walked several feet behind them before speaking.

"Hey old man, if you don't want any trouble, give me what's in that purse and in your wallet."

He ignored the predator and kept walking, noticing a picket fence in front of the house up ahead.

"Hey old man, I'm talking to you. Do you hear me?"

"Yes I do sir. Give me one second, please."

And with that, Paul calmly told his sister-in-law to step to the side of the walkway. He reached toward the picket fence and pulled out one of the loose posts quickly and swung as hard as he could, nail face out, still in the wood. He swung it right at his assailant's face. The nail pierced the cheek of the thug; blood spurting onto the sidewalk. He pulled back and swung again and again, six times in all, puncturing their friendly neighbor's skin each time, until the assailant finally had enough and ran off.

"You're a crazy old man," he screamed as he ran off.

"Thanks Paul," said his sister-in-law matter of factly.

And they started off to the eye doctor as if nothing had happened, until Paul thought better of it. I better ring the doorbell and let them know I had to borrow their post, he thought. As he approached the door, it opened quickly. The young woman who opened the door smiled broadly and spoke loudly, "Thank you so much for running off that piece of garbage. That was awesome. My name is Tina Boyle. Do you mind if I ask you a few questions?"

"No, sorry," he said, "we need to get to the doctor. Nice meeting you, Tina. I just wanted to give you back your fence. Thank you so much for allowing me to use it. Perhaps we'll run into each other another day."

"My pleasure," she answered laughing and shaking her head, as they headed down the street to the doctor.

The next day I decided to buy the New York Daily News, which was not something I did often. I read an article in the neighborhood beat section by a writer named Tina Boyle. It spoke of an incident in Brooklyn where an elderly gentleman confronted an assailant and sent

149

him cowering off. I showed it to my wife, who immediately called her mother to warn her of the dangers of "the hood". Citing this story, Nancy said it was imperative that her parents move out of Brooklyn immediately and in with us.

When informed of his daughter's concern, her father laughed robustly just like he would when tossing Jillian in the air. "I think I can take care of myself okay. For your information, that was me in that article, Nancy."

But that was one of the last times that he was able to show off his strength, his power and his zest. For shortly after that incident, he started to lose weight and sleep a lot. He no longer was eating that second and third portion at dinner. In short, he was starting to melt away. He was eighty-four years old and finally he was tired.

If you punch in the words "Todd Shipyards" into an Internet search engine, one of the first things you notice is the many advertisements for personal injury lawyers. You see, the workers at the yard had been exposed to asbestos for many years and were developing higher than normal cancer rates. And finally, at eighty four years old, it was Grandpa Paul's turn.

He would lie in his hospital bed most of the days, with an occasional walk down the hall with his walker. We debated whether to bring Jillian along for a visit and finally decided it might brighten Grandpa's spirits. When we arrived at his room with Jillian, he was sitting in a chair, kind of out of it. Little two-year-old Jillian sprinted towards him, jumped as high as she could, twisted in the air and landed in his lap. I cringed. He was so frail. But before we could correct Jillian, he summoned all his strength and gave her a little toss in the air. They both laughed wildly.

And so it went, as Grandpa closed out his life. Jillian would visit and jump in his lap or climb over the rails of his hospital bed to use it as a trampoline or just to cuddle with him. And that little kid made her grandfather happy. Until finally one Sunday night he was too tired to go on, so he said goodbye. And he died.

I breathed deeply, then looked out the window. A Cardinal, the reddest bird I have ever seen, flew down from the sky, landed on the window sill and whistled a goodbye salute.

Grandma moved up to live with Nancy and me shortly after Grandpa Paul's death. And as we would sit around the table, sometimes we would reminisce about Grandpa; about his funny, endearing old-fashioned ways and we would laugh.

"You know Grandpa comes back sometimes," Jillian would chime in on these occasions, with a broad smile on her little face. And that would make everyone else smile and laugh even more. Indeed, when we talked of Grandpa, it did bring him back in a way; he lived on in our talk, in our descriptions, in the pictures we all have in our minds.

On October 12, it was Nancy and my anniversary, the very first one without Grandpa around. Both my wife and mother-in-law were a little down, thinking how much they missed him. They both lay in bed that morning, both a bit depressed. We needed some groceries; so Jillian and I went out early to the Supermarket and picked up some things.

The store was empty. I picked up some eggs, milk and bread, along with Cheerios for my little companion. Once I loaded up the cart with all our pickings, I pushed my cart toward the checkout counter with my right hand, and held Jillian against my chest with my left hand. As Jillian and I moved forward, she peered down the aisle in the opposite direction, over my shoulder.

Before I could start loading up the goods onto the checkout counter, Jillian spoke to someone behind me. "Hi," she said with a wave of her hand and a gentle giggle. I turned around and looked down the long aisle. I saw no one; the aisle was empty, eerily still.

So I started to load up the groceries on the conveyor belt at the checkout, quickly checking my pockets whether I would have enough cash or would have to pay with my credit card. Jillian continued to stare down the aisle over my shoulder. Again she giggled, waved her hand and blurted out, "Hi." I looked down the aisle again; no one was there.

"Jillian, who did you say just hello to?"

"Grandpa," she answered without a moment of hesitation, pointing straight ahead. "He's right there."

I looked down the aisle again. Again, it was still; like right before a summer thunderstorm, when all around you seems like a still, black and white photograph, a frozen moment. And no one was there; there was absolutely no sign of life at all down that grocery aisle. In fact, it seemed like we were the only customers in the store.

"Are you sure that's him? What is he wearing?" I asked, puzzled.

"The scratchy red shirt he likes with the checks on it, black pants and white socks."

My mind raced and I was more dumbfounded than ever. Jillian had just aptly described, in her own simple words, the red flannel shirt he used to wear all the time. And just like she said, he always seemed to wear white socks when he wasn't getting dressed up.

"Does he want to say anything to us?" I asked.

Jillian looked down the vacant aisle for a second as if listening to someone. She paused and nodded. Then she informed me, "He said Hi, he just wants to say hi. He has to go now; but he will be around; he's always around. He comes back sometimes, you know."

And those words were uplifting. When we would talk of Grandpa, Jillian always said he comes back sometimes; but I always thought she was talking figuratively, that he came back in our words. But Jillian meant what she said. Indeed, he comes back sometimes! Jillian's Grandpa used to tell us to be afraid of the living, not the dead. The dead won't hurt you, he said, they will only help you along. And I again recalled his incident in Brooklyn, memorialized in the Daily News. Fear the living, not the dead. That is very good advice.

Jillian and I went home and I wasn't sure whether to tell my wife about her father's visit with Jillian or not. As I debated whether or not to tell her, I looked out into the backyard where Jillian was standing right next to her swing set with the crusts of her toast from breakfast in her hand.

Like a lot of kids, she never ate the crusts. But it was odd that she would bring her leftovers outside with her, I thought. So I watched to see what she would do. She stood motionless for about twenty seconds. Then, all of a sudden, she extended her hand straight out with her palm to the sky with the bread resting on top. A second later, a bright red Cardinal landed in her hand, taking the scraps of bread from her. And just as quickly, the bird flew off. Jillian laughed. And I decided that I should tell her mother all about Grandpa's visit with Jillian after all.

Superfly Meets Richard Cory

All nightmares are dreams, but not all dreams are nightmares.

Based on a true story of a boy who realized a dream to play in the NBA for the New York Knicks; to sink last-second jump shots at Madison Square Garden and to be cheered by 19,000 frenzied fans.

Superfly Meets Richard Cory

Whenever Richard Cory went down town,
We people on the pavement looked at him;
He was a gentleman from sole to crown,
Clean-favoured and imperially slim.

And he was always quietly arrayed,
And he was always human when he talked;
But still he fluttered pulses when he said,
"Good Morning!" and he glittered when he walked.

And he was rich, yes, richer than a king,
And admirably schooled in every grace;
In fine -- we thought that he was everything
To make us wish that we were in his place.

So on we worked and waited for the light,
And went without the meat and cursed the bread,
And Richard Cory, one calm summer night,
Went home and put a bullet in his head.

Edward Arlington Robinson wrote those words over a century ago. I

read them as a high school kid and remember my heart dropping like a

roller coaster car into my stomach the first time I read that fourth

stanza. But as I get older I am seeing that you don't have to drill a

bullet into your head to destroy your own life. There are plenty of

other ways to do it; putting a bullet in your head is just the quickest and most dramatic. This is a story about someone who tried very hard to kill himself, but failed. His name is Supe.

"I never asked to be nobody's hero," Supe said quietly to me.

And that statement hit me; not hard, but subtly like a tap on the shoulder. All these years I wished I could be someone like him; to have people admire me for what I could do. And all along he just wanted to be someone like me; to fit in and have a chance to be himself for a little stretch.

I have covered sports for newspapers almost thirty years, and to this day, I never saw anyone with such promise as a basketball player as Supe Wilson. Many years ago, in the 1970s, it seemed Supe was everyone's hero. He was the coolest kid anyone ever saw; an outright legend by the time he was 17 years old. His freshman year in High School, he was a skinny runt of about 5 feet 10 inches, with a funkedelic Afro that made him look about a foot taller. And he could play basketball with a style and flair like no one in his neighborhood had ever seen. And in his neighborhood in Northern Philadelphia, people had seen some enormously fine basketball players. He was the point guard that year, the starting point guard, on one of the best high school basketball teams in the country and only in ninth grade. He wasn't silky or smooth like a ballet dancer; he was jerky and frenetic, a blur of funk and jazz amidst a court filled with opponents who played like clumsy classical instruments. When he dribbled the ball it moved back and forth, between his legs, around his back and up the court in a blur, always finding its way into a teammate's hands for an uncontested lay-up.

Every basketball game was a party back then, a place for the community to strut its stuff and show its collective pride; every game was a packed house, standing room only. Everyone wanted to see Supe and the rest of his team play. And college coaches would show up, not just local Philly guys, but coaches from all over the country; and they would sit in that cold, ratty old gym with the locals, just to watch the games and sneak in a word to the kids about their school. And the locals would dream; dream about maybe one of these kids breaking out from this place and becoming a big shot, maybe even making it in the NBA.

Back then you couldn't dunk the ball, it was against the rules. But Supe's team routinely would win by forty points or more; so sometimes, when the game was safely in the bag, Supe would lob the ball a foot or two above the rim to his friend, Jimmy Beech. And Jimmy would slam the ball through the hole, his Afro blowing backward like it was in a hurricane. And then Jimmy would hang on the rim and do a pull-up, as if to put an exclamation mark on the festivities. And Supe and Jimmy would holler and whoop up the crowd into a frenzy. Of course, they both were then booted from the game and their team assessed a technical foul. And Coach Martin would go nuts; screaming his lungs out at them. But Supe and Jimmy didn't care a bit. The show was what mattered; they were the heroes of the community, black and proud. And nobody had their style and flamboyance.

And next year and the year after, it only got better out on the court for Supe. Between his freshman and sophomore years he grew from 5 feet 10 inches tall up to 6 feet 7 inches tall. And even though he grew so fast, he still maintained his coordination, speed and agility. He could dribble, shoot, pass and rebound. And no one could run and jump like him. He could do whatever he wanted on the court and he did. He did things we never saw before. Teammates were constantly getting sprained fingers from the unexpected passes he made to them; passes from improbable and impossible angles, around his back, over, under and around dumbfounded defenders. He was a High School All-American both his Junior and Senior years; and sought by every university with a major basketball program.

And when he sauntered into the gymnasium like a proud rooster, everyone stopped and things got quiet. He modeled his persona after Superfly, the movie character, the King of the Slums. That's why he was called Supe, short for Superfly. And because he could do anything on the basketball court, people loved him. They loved him so much they were willing to overlook all the darkness off the court.

Supe lived in the Richard Allen projects; the biggest housing projects in the north end of the City of Philadelphia. Like other inner-city housing projects, it had its problems. But the Richard Allen projects seemed even bleaker than the typical project. Richard Allen is concentrated in an eight block radius with few stores or few anything for that matter, nearby. And because of that isolation, it is a closed world, a city within a city, where the positive elements of city life rarely peek through the cracks in the black clouds that seem to hover ominously over Richard Allen. The crime, the violence, the drugs are so concentrated; such a pervasive a part of everyday life, that you cannot escape them.

A two bedroom apartment in these projects was where Supe, his mom and his seven siblings called home, same as Bill Cosby did years before them. Only the Richard Allen Homes of Supe were a lot meaner and dangerous than the Richard Allen Homes of Bill Cosby and Fat Albert. Time was not kind to the residents of Richard Allen; drugs and all the residual problems they created had turned a place where people could live into a place where people just survived. The physical decay of the project was apparent enough, but the lack of hope among the residents was what made life there even more desolate. Almost everyone was on welfare, and Supe's family was no exception. Supe never met his father and that bothered him, although he would never let on that it did. There was little, if any money for luxury; no television, just a radio and

163

a telephone. And Supe slept on a mattress on the floor because a bed was out of the question; simply too expensive.

Besides that mattress on the floor, Supe had two possessions that he could call his own in that apartment while growing up; an old weathered basketball and a poster of New York Knicks guard Walt Frazier taped to the wall. Despite living in Philadelphia, Supe was a diehard Knick fan. And he especially loved Frazier and his backcourt mate Earl Monroe. He loved their style, their confidence, their swagger. When he practiced on the playground near his home, he always pretended to be Frazier or Monroe playing on their home court: Madison Square Garden in New York.

And although despair filled the air, basketball gave Supe and his buddies hope. It seemed to give them life. But basketball was also a curse. It nurtured some very bad habits. Supe was the hope for his whole family and his whole community. He was just a kid and he was supposed to look after all his younger brothers and sisters as well as be the star. And he was smart enough to figure out that if you cut some corners you could get things you wanted or needed with very little effort. He was big, strong and powerful and not afraid to shake down his classmates for a little protection money when he needed pocket change. He didn't lament or feel any guilt over that either; in fact, he kind of relished his status as a tough guy. And because of his basketball ability, his status as the best of the best, he never had to answer for his actions. He would get caught smoking weed or drinking beer behind school, but he knew he would never be suspended because the team needed him, the school needed him, and the community needed him. He was their hope. So everyone pretended he was a good kid because he was one of the few sure things they knew in their world. If they were doomed to the projects, at least Supe would get out of this rat's nest. And when he became famous in the NBA they could all say I knew him way back when he was a kid.

His family couldn't afford a bed for him, yet one day Supe showed up at school driving a Cadillac. We all knew where it came from, some booster for some big-time college program; maybe Kentucky, maybe Maryland or maybe Tennessee, nobody knew for sure which one, and Supe certainly wasn't talking about it. And his clothes all of a sudden were stylish and flashy; no longer Salvation Army duds but fashionable expensive threads, jackets made out of real leather. Supe even started to have cash in his senior year; more cash than he could have ever shaken down from his classmates. And the amazing thing was nobody seemed to care that it was wrong; nobody told Supe to straighten up, to toe the line and do things by the book. So he never did. He just went along with it because nobody ever said no to him. He just did whatever he wanted; no boundaries, no limits and no father.

And when it came time for Supe to pick a college, he chose Kentucky, who was always in the running to be the National Champions. When he announced his intentions, it was big news in the Bluegrass State. Supe would be the cornerstone of the Kentucky juggernaut for the next four years, they announced, to much fanfare. But a funny thing happened on the road to Lexington, Kentucky. On August 26th, when the rest of the Kentucky student body was signing up for their classes; Supe was nowhere to be found. He wasn't on campus anywhere; not in his dorm, certainly not in the library and not in the gym. In fact, no one knew where to find him. The coaches were going out of their minds. Where was Supe? They called his home, but neither his mom nor any of his siblings knew where he was.

Where was he? He was getting high with a couple of friends in another building at the project; just kicking back and relaxing. And the more he thought about it, the more he realized he didn't want to be all the way out in Kentucky anyways, no matter how much money the boosters there might funnel his way. He wanted to be near his boys and near his family. He was a hip city kid, funk ran through his veins; he didn't want to spend four years in bluegrass country listening to redneck cowboy music. So he decided he wouldn't show up at Kentucky, he would stay closer to Philly and go to school somewhere else. The next day he got in his car, rode across town to LaSalle University and enrolled there. LaSalle was not a big basketball powerhouse, but it was Division I nonetheless. So what if they hadn't had a winning season in a few years; he would single-handedly turn it around, he thought. Hey, it didn't matter where he went anyways; it would just be two or three years and then he would head off to the NBA.

The folks at LaSalle could hardly believe their good fortune. They immediately went from the basement to the penthouse. And all the dreams of a small, city school were tied to the local kid, the 6'7'' left-handed phenomenon with the sweet mid-range jumper and the passing skills of a point guard. The preseason hyped the local kid as the savior of the program, the herald of a new era. It was an uplifting story with a local flavor and it made good copy for the Philadelphia sportswriters. The local kid turns his back on the national powerhouse to stay home and be one of us. There was a lot of pressure on Supe, but he delivered; he delivered big-time, on the court at least. He averaged nineteen points, ten rebounds and six assists a game as a freshman. The team won 25 games and was ranked as high as twelfth nationally. He was selected as a Second Team All American and led the team to its first NCAA tournament since the 1950's.

But just like momma told me as a kid, if something looks too good to be true, it probably is. Such was the case with Supe. His seemingly idyllic life was, in reality, a total mess. His two brothers didn't have his knack on the hardwood, but they sure had his knack for stirring up trouble. Supe always had to be the one to bail them out. And his Mom was in failing health, so it was left for him to watch out for his brothers and sisters when she went to the Hospital. And he actually tried to keep up with his schoolwork at first, until he realized he would be passed right through if he just took the right courses; the courses from the professors friendly to the basketball program. And there was a lot of pressure; which led him to get high a lot, just to release stress, he assured himself.

Supe sure had some bad habits. In addition to, or perhaps as a result of, his propensity to get high, he missed practices and got in fights with his teammates. The older guys on the team resented all the special rules for Supe. They all wore ties on road trips. They had to show for practice. They had to keep up their grades. Who did this freshman think he was? Sure, he was the best player anyone had ever seen, but he had not a chip, but a granite block, on his shoulder. Out on the court he was the best, great to play with. He shared the ball and worked hard on defense. He made everyone else a better player. But he was not a nice guy; he was always irritable, always in a foul mood. And the local kids he hung out with were more important to him than the team, it seemed. He never joined the others in any social setting off the court. It was like he thought he was too good, at least it seemed to that way to his teammates.

So on it went like this for two more years. The team was good; great actually and nationally ranked, but Supe was the only blue-chipper. When they played the really good, elite teams, their weak point guards were pressed all game long, by waves and waves of more talented players. So even that task of breaking the press eventually fell on Supe. And when the NCAA tournament rolled around, the more talented teams, with their big-dollar facilities and budgets had enough fire-power to eclipse Supe's individual star power. And it led to even more frustration and more surliness on the part of Supe. So after his junior year, Supe threw his hat into the NBA draft and was picked up in the first round by the New York Knicks.

How fortunate was that? Supe would get to play in "The World's Most Famous Arena", Madison Square Garden on 33rd Street in the middle of the "Greatest City in The World". Supe would get to play for Red Holzman, who had coached Walt Frazier, Willis Reed and Earl Monroe and who had two championship rings to his name. The Garden was the place of Supe's basketball dreams; the place he imagined when he hit that last second shot while practicing on the playground, the place he imagined his name being called when they announced the starting lineup. The NBA was Supe's destiny and he would get to play on the largest stage of all. It all seemed so right.

And, once in the NBA, the basketball part of it was still easy for Supe. Even though he was a frontcourt player, his ball-handling and passing skills allowed him to handle the ball in the Knicks half court sets. This allowed the Knicks over-sized guards to post up near the basket and score on smaller opponents. The "point forward", a frontcourt player bearing the brunt of the ball-handling, was a new innovation in the early 1980's. Supe, along with several other young and talented players like him throughout the league, popularized this new more fluid approach to the game. They showed that tall frontcourt players could be just as agile as their smaller counterparts in the backcourt. Supe averaged thirteen points, six rebounds and five assists a game; not too shabby for a rookie. And the Knicks made the playoffs in his first year, after failing to make the playoffs the previous four years.

Off the court; however, the transition to the pros was not as smooth. Supe's family continued to have problems back in Philly; problems that he would always have to handle, since he was the oldest and his mother was dieing. And despite all the money he was paid, he still seemed to always be broke. He simply didn't have the discipline to hold onto his money. He had his big house in New Jersey and he constantly had to lend a hand to all his friends and family.

And he liked to party. In the big city, with all its temptations, with a couple of young teammates by his side who also liked to live large, he was doomed to succumb to the debauchery that persistently presented itself to him. There was always some facilitator there to sidle up to Supe and his new young millionaire friends. Sure, there were some older players who lived a little more frugally, a little more slowly and they would warn the younger players to slow down. This is a short career, they would say, take care of your bodies so you can make it last longer. But the young turks paid no mind. They were young, rich and filled with hubris, the playoff bound heroes of New York City; they were the young Knicks, the new breed, and no one could tell them what to do. No one knew better than them.

By the end of the year, the hard life he was leading started to catch up with him and the lackluster pattern started: hung-over practices, missed practices, even hung-over for games. And in his second year he was equally successful on the court, showing flashes of even greater promise. But the problem was he was not on the court enough; he was injured or missing for undisclosed personal reasons. There were always excuses. He was inconsistent, not dependable, not the kind of employee you need to make a run at the NBA championship. He had plenty of talent, but he wasn't as focused as he should have been; he didn't take care of himself. And after five years of this, of constantly trying to cajole him to reach for his potential, the Knick brass finally gave up on Supe; they traded him to the last place Cleveland Cavaliers.

Supe didn't last long there; at the time, all the Cavaliers did was lose. And their coach was a screamer, trying to coax wins from a talent-less team filled with malcontents. There was nothing but frustration in Cleveland; Supe's talent was there but his mind wasn't. But the money kept coming and the good times continued to roll. When confronted by his new coach about a cocaine problem, Supe informed his coach that it wasn't a problem at all; he had plenty of money to pay for the stuff.

That response was the last straw and it ended his time in Cleveland. "Get out of here loser. I'll make sure you never work again in this league you lowlife," bellowed his coach.

But despite the promise of his Cleveland coach, Supe got another chance. If you have enough potential in anything, it seems there is always someone ready to give you another chance, to overlook your obvious flaws. So Supe made one final stop, in Philadelphia, where it all started. And there was hope that the local boy would come home and finally live up to his vast potential and lead the locals to the crown. But, alas, he only lasted twelve games; after badly tearing cartilage in his knee, his basketball career was over. He was 27 years old.

What do you do when the thing you know how to do best is taken from you? What do you do when you become obsolete? He had never planned for anything; basketball had always provided. Basketball was always his comfort, the solution to all his problems. Now it was gone.

So he coasted, not knowing how to move on from the glory, blowing through whatever money he hadn't already squandered. And by the age of 31, he was out of money and working on an assembly line. He didn't have the skills to do much else, he never graduated from college and he never held a real job other than basketball. And because he had never been held accountable for anything before, he had trouble taking direction. And he missed a lot of days, too hung over to get out of bed, and that never goes over too well with the boss whether you are making a million dollars a year as a starting forward or $3.25 an hour on the assembly line.

He lived with his girlfriend and his son for many years. But it wasn't a love story. There were fights and violence. When he drank, Supe had no reluctance to work out his frustration by battering his girlfriend or son. And the beating went on for years and years until finally, after years of leniency and minor brushes with the law, a judge finally said enough is enough and threatened him with jail-time. It seems, after years of abuse, his girlfriend had kicked him out and obtained a court order prohibiting him from seeing her and their son. But Supe ignored the order; after all, rules didn't apply to him, or so he thought. So he visited her during one of his cocaine benders and held her against her will for a day and a half. And this time it was different. The judge didn't see a basketball star before him, he just saw someone who had visited his girlfriend against a court order, repeatedly threatened her , beat her and held her against her will. He saw a guy with a string of DUI convictions who ignored each and every warning. He saw nothing but a punk and a bully.

Supe's lawyer told him Judge Thomas means business this time; that these were serious charges that he would have difficulty defending. And for one of the first times in his life, Supe got it. He became reflective; he thought about himself and all he had done and he admitted something to himself. He finally admitted his failure. He went before Judge Thomas and was contrite. He pleaded guilty to all charges and was sentenced to three years in prison.

Now, a year later, as I sat across from Supe, I looked at him in his orange prison jumpsuit and thought it was such a humiliation that he landed here in prison. "I guess you realize you're not anybody's hero anymore," I said to him.

"That's not entirely true," he said. "The guys in here still look up to me for some weird reason, but now I'm comfortable with that. They look up to me, but it's not like before, we're all sort of the same in here because we're all screw-ups."

He swallowed hard and slowly, looked at me and continued, "You know, I'm not angry anymore. I was so damn angry, so damn long and I hurt a lot of people because I was so irritated about everything. But the person I hurt most was myself. Jail was the best thing for me. It got me away from things, away from the drugs and booze and all the demands and expectations that messed me up in the first place. The only person I have to blame for being here is me. I take full responsibility; I deserve to be here. This place isn't lavish, but the good thing about being here is the only person I have to take care of is me. And there isn't anyone looking to me expecting anything."

As he spoke, I recalled the poem I read in high school; when sensibility was nonsensical, when little things had immense importance and when essential things seemed not so essential. I had the luxury of being stupid and making mistakes, of skinning my knees and getting up without anyone watching me under a microscope. I had the luxury of being a kid because I didn't have seven siblings to watch out for. I had the luxury of being a kid because I didn't have the hopes and dreams of my entire community dropped onto my shoulders to carry around every hour of every day. And I had a father. I had a father who loved me and cared for me enough to discipline me, to say no sometimes. Soon I realized I wasn't talking to Superfly; I was talking to Richard Cory.

"Hey Supe, did you ever read the poem Richard Cory in High School or College?"

"Not in school, in here; I read it here in jail. I used to be just like Richard Cory, you know. I had everything; money, fame and adulation, just like him. I couldn't handle it either; couldn't get myself together."

If you use a bullet to try and kill yourself, you almost always are successful and it is over quickly. But when you use drugs and booze to kill yourself, it can take years. It's drawn-out that way; less dramatic, but often even more devastating and more tragic. I guess going through life numbed and altered by external substances is less painful than having to be a hero all the time; a meal ticket, always having to live up to the expectations of others and always having to pull something out from inside you that you aren't sure is in there in the first place. It was heartbreaking to me that Supe was here in jail; but by the same token, he was not scattered, angry and frenetic like he used to be. He seemed grounded and comfortable with himself, almost serene; not some movie caricature of the King of the Streets trying to keep it "real" for his "boyz".

"What are you going to do when you get out of here?" I asked.

"I'm just going to live. I am not going to strive for perfection; I am going to strive for contentment. I'm going to get a job and live clean without booze and drugs and violence and anger and just be myself. I'm going to look at the sun rise every morning and be happy I have another day. Maybe I'll even finish my degree up. I could do that now; I'm a lot smarter and patient now than I was when I was twenty. This place taught me that. All you have is time here, so you either go crazy or you face yourself and get yourself together. So I'm not a hero anymore, thank goodness. Now I can be what I always wanted to be anyways, a regular person. You know I lost a lot over the years. I lost my big house and all my cars, I lost touch with my kid, I blew hundreds of thousands of dollars and it probably seems to you like I have nothing now. I'm just a jerk who blew everything and ended up in prison, a loser. But I feel better than ever now; I feel like I did getting out of high school, when all was possible. You know, I feel like I found something here in jail. I found a person, a person I could grow to like, inside of me. Jail is more freedom than when I was Superfly, playing in the NBA, living the life. Back then everyone wanted a piece of me and, even though I'm six feet seven inches tall, there weren't enough pieces of me to go around for everybody. In jail, I started really looking at myself for the first time and living just for me. Jail made me wiser and now I'm ready to get back and finally contribute something more than just putting the ball in the hoop; not because I have to, but because I want to."

"How do you spend your time here, why do you say you are wiser?" I asked.

"I read and I think. I read anything that strikes me at the time; Stephen King one day, the Bible another day, Anton Chekhov another day. I like those Russian authors a lot; I like their style and the way they analyze stuff; they look at the heart of the problem, they're very direct, very intense. Sometimes I play ball in the yard; I'm still the best guy out there by a long shot, even though I'm almost 50, but I'm sore the next day after playing, so I only play about once or twice a week. I'm not trying to run away from myself any more or impress anyone with how street-real I am. I do what I want to do now and I got rid of all my resentment. That's how I'm wiser."

And as I bade farewell to Supe, I concluded that his landing in jail was not such a tragedy after all. Life is funny and paradoxical. Supe could have had anything he wanted, except what he really wanted; structure, contentment and peace. The man who seemed to have all the freedom in the world had to go to jail to become liberated; to be free to be himself. I asked Supe if he had it all to do again would he change anything.

He smiled and answered, "No nothing, nothing at all. Except I do wish I hadn't been so violent; but I think I'm over that now. I'm a 48 year old work in progress who is actually making progress. My life is what it is and I'm okay with that. I've seen the view from the penthouse and I've seen the view from the gutter. I got to play in Madison Square Garden, the Greatest Arena in the World. I got to hear my name announced and hear 19,000 people scream for me. How many people get to see life from all those different perspectives? In a crazy way I'm kind of lucky, don't you think?"

Three months after my visit with Supe, he was paroled. He served sixteen months of his three year sentence. I figured I might read about him relapsing in the paper one day; that he would be back in trouble soon enough. After all, Supe and trouble seemed to go together like bacon and eggs. But a year went by and then another. And after three years, I still hadn't read or heard anything of Supe. By this time I had taken a job in Atlanta and I didn't get to Philly that often. So I decided to track him down with a quick Google search. Sorting through all the accolades of his basketball career, I found he was employed right where he grew up, at the new Community Center near the Richard

Allen projects. I resolved to visit him the next time I was in Philadelphia to cover a game.

Two months later, I was in town covering the Atlanta Hawks game against the Philadelphia 76ers. When I dropped by the Community Center to say hello to Supe, that January afternoon, he greeted me warmly; thanking me for visiting him in prison. He looked fit as he refereed a game of ten year olds playing basketball. He told me he was taking courses at night towards his degree, reading voraciously and attending Alcoholics Anonymous meetings on a regular basis. He told me he was happy. Then, he introduced me to Eugene, a bright ten year old kid. Supe told me Eugene liked to read and play sports and that he dreamed of being a sportswriter someday. It seems Eugene doesn't have a father or a mother; he lives with Supe, his foster parent, who is trying to adopt him.

"Eugene," Supe said. "Meet my friend Steven. He's a sportswriter. If you need a role model, look no further than Steve. He can tell you all you need to know about being a writer and also a little bit about being a man. I wish I had been more like Steve in my younger days."

Supe then smiled at me, warmly and genuinely.

"Supe," I said with a grin, "I never asked to be nobody's hero."

"Yeah, okay, I hear you on that, Richard Cory; being a hero ain't nothin' but trouble. Nobody, absolutely nobody, knows that better than me," he chuckled.

"Who is Richard Cory, Coach?" asked Eugene, "I thought your friend was named Steve."

"Richard Cory is someone Steve and I both know, Gene. Richard Cory is, as they say, a real character. C'mon lets shoot around. Steve come on, join us."

So Supe and I played two on two against Gene and one of his friends. We played for almost an hour and Supe and I became kids again, forgetting everything going on in the adult world and just basking in the joy of bouncing a leather ball and shooting it through a metal hoop.

We let Gene's team beat us 21-19. When Gene hit the last shot to win the game, Supe beamed with a broad smile. And I felt happy for Supe. Even though he lost this game of two on two against a couple of ten year olds, he was delighted. Supe was finally content, and finally winning in a much larger way on a much smaller stage. And he was winning at a much bigger game than basketball.

To Dream of 800

Never admire anyone too deeply; you will usually end up disappointed.

To Dream of 800

The summer has come; the year is 2031. Sister Hannah lives with her children in the Brooklyn district of Bedford Stuyvesant, a neighborhood of roughly three square miles once described to me by a local psychiatrist as having one of the most severe cases of schizophrenia he had ever observed. On one block in the North part of the neighborhood, you might find an idyllic tree-lined block, populated by elegant century-old brownstone row houses, with graceful oak and mahogany parlors, high ceilings and detailed Victorian handiwork throughout. The residents of these homes are well-educated and well-heeled; families headed by doctors, college professors, artists and writers. Not far to the South, however, you might come upon an entirely different scene- a bleak public housing project filled with all the ills that seem to infect such developments: despair, crime, unemployment and other related sorts of unsavory and unhealthy conditions all around you.

Sister Hannah has raised foster kids in this neighborhood for 44 years. She started her operation in 1987, only barely into her 20s, inspired by Sister Mary Jude, the nun who had raised her in this very same neighborhood. She worked hard, acting as mother, father, teacher, protector and friend to all her children. She was widely known as a miracle worker of sorts, somehow taking the toughest kids from the toughest projects and the bleakest situations and rounding them into authentic citizens; active participants in upbeat endeavors and bona fide contributors to society.

She started out her mission in shelters donated by the Brooklyn Diocese; but since 2015, she was fortunate to be able to raise her children in a beautiful four story brownstone on 200 Greene Avenue, right down the street from Von King Park. A wealthy benefactor had generously bought the home for her and continued to pay all the maintenance, taxes and utilities. That was good; she was better at the work of charity than the work of fundraising, maintenance and bookkeeping. In the first few years, she often had to worry about money a lot. It had been a blessing that the administrative burdens had been lifted from her shoulders.   She could concentrate on her real

work.

Most all of Sister's kids who graduated from her care still wrote her

letters or sent her e-mails telling her how they were doing; how their

lives were turning out. And she kept all the correspondence; letters

organized in shoe boxes and e-mails organized in neat electronic

directories in the memory of her computer. When she would sometimes

get discouraged and tired, Sister would read these communications.

They would lift her up and energize her to keep up with the current

batch of kids. At 66 years old, this motivational reading was the spark

she needed and it was relied upon more than ever it seemed. But,

despite her advancing years, she still was pretty sturdy and very adept

at keeping the kids in line, helping them to follow their enlightened

instincts and ignore the disturbed call of the streets.

This current crew was a good bunch of kids. They ranged in age from

thirteen to eighteen. All ten boys were a little rough around the edges;

but they all showed promise in their own particular approach to life.

Each had a skill, a special talent that made them unique. For instance, thirteen-year old Lamar was an artist who now channeled his propensity for producing graffiti into more worthwhile art projects at school. Sixteen-year old Joe was a scholar who had a love of analytic geometry and physics. And Al was an accomplished jazz musician and point guard extraordinaire. But Marcus, at eighteen, the oldest of the group, was the one with the most promise; the one who was gifted in so many ways. You see, Marcus could do just about anything he set his mind to and he was the most determined and driven child Sister had ever raised.

Marcus had been with Sister since he was three years old, when his 21-year old Mom was killed by a stray bullet meant for a local thug and self proclaimed "hip hop entrepreneur" named Def Vader. Marcus' dad, as far as he knew, left the scene before he was even born; and, despite his difficult circumstances, Marcus was the most focused child Sister had ever seen. Marcus was one of those kids who always did everything right; he followed directions, did his schoolwork, helped his classmates and cared for his body. Whatever he was doing, there was always purpose to it. He had grown to an impressive height of six feet, four inches tall and was a chiseled 215 pounds. His hair was closely cropped to his head and he was always neat. And he had a presence, that special gift that few possess- the gift to enter a room and have all heads turn and gawk at you because they know something about you is special. He looked like a movie star; a younger version of Denzel Washington; streetwise, yet sophisticated and polished all at once. He was headed to Stanford University in California next fall, to study political science and run track. He was the New York City PSAL Champion at 100, 200 and 400 meters, as well as the long jump. The track coach out at Stanford thought Marcus could be the next great American Decathlete; that is if he could keep the Stanford football coach at bay. The football coach saw him more as a wide receiver than an Olympian.

But the thing Marcus loved to do more than either run track or play football was to play pick-up baseball with his friends down the street at Von King Park. In fact, playing baseball was the one thing all Sister's boys loved to do together. And before bed these long summer days, they would all sit around the television and watch the Amazing One, Centerfielder Phil Perry of the San Diego Padres. Sister encouraged them to watch him, it kept them off the street; but more than that, she could see that Phil inspired the kids to dream big. And kids dreaming big was what kept her going at this special little gig of hers.

Legend was that Phil Perry grew up just like these kids in the Brooklyn foster care system, with no Mom or Dad. He learned to love baseball playing pickup at Tompkins Park, before it was re-named Von King Park, just like these kids. And now after seventeen years in the Big Leagues, averaging roughly 50 home runs a year, after recently surpassing the record of 788 homers set by the great Yankee third baseman, Alex Rodriguez, Phil was going to be the first man to hit 800 home runs. And it looked like it would happen soon, in this very summer of 2031.

One night Al said to the group assembled around the television, "Wouldn't it be great to see Phil hit number 800?" He has 798 now and he will be in New York next week, playing the Mets!"

Marcus chided him. "How are we going to get tickets; all the corporate types have scoffed up all the seats. We're just a bunch of kids from Bed-Stuy."

Sister, overhearing the conversation, said, "Do you want to go see Phil Perry play, boys? The man who bought this house for us has some connections with Major League Baseball, you know. How about I ask him for some tickets? Most of you have never seen a Major League game have you?"

"No, Sister. But that would be excellent," said Marcus, beaming.

"Okay boys. Then it's a date. I'll ask my friend for eleven tickets. We will be able to see all the games too. My friend can get us seats for the entire Mets- Padres series. If he hits number 800 in New York this weekend, I guarantee you guys will be there to see it."

"All right," they all screamed, slapping each other with "high fives". The game they watched that Tuesday night on television was the Padres against the Phillies, the last game before the three game series with the Mets. In the bottom of the ninth, with the Padres down by two runs, Perry hit a three run homer to win the game. He had 799 career home runs, only one more for 800. The boys listened to the ancient announcer and former Met Ron Darling talk about Perry in reverential terms. "I started in the Majors about fifty years ago as a player and have had the grand and glorious fortune to see some of the greatest players who ever played this game, this glorious pastime of our republic. I saw Mark McGwire and Barry Bonds, muscles juiced up on steroids, each smack 70 home runs in a season. We all thought, after the advent of the Expobalco spit detection test, the test that made it possible to detect steroids in saliva, that we would never see another man approach 800 home runs. But we were all wrong. Phil Perry, the stray kid from Brooklyn, New York, who grew up as a poor kid in foster homes, showed us that anything is possible; that you can come from nothing and reach the stars. What a great story. Perry is now headed back to his hometown, New York, to see if he can hit number 800."

The boys all beamed with pride. Phil Perry was one of them, a Brooklyn boy made good. They all looked up to him because he gave life to their dreams. Sister would say anything is possible and Phil Perry was her corroboration; he grew up just like these kids, right here in Bed-Stuy, without a Mom or Dad or a nickel to his name.

"To bed fellas," yelled Sister, "The game is over. If you want to go see Phil Perry play this weekend, you will get your bottoms up in those beds of yours, pronto."

"Good night Sister," they all yelled as they rushed upstairs. Each boy went upstairs quickly, almost sprinting, because they all knew one thing. They all knew that Sister meant business about not taking them to the game if they didn't go up to bed immediately.

Marcus thought about where he was going as he lay awake in bed that night, staring at the streak of light illuminating his ceiling through the window, and he was a little frightened. He would miss Sister out in California, he knew that. But she would still touch him. He knew he would be like those other people who lived with her in the past, sending e-mails and letters to keep her informed about their lives. He loved Sister. Sister was always there to help with his problems, whatever they were. She was always there to listen to him; she had a way of making him feel important. That was the good side of living here with her. The downside was that she was always in control because she always followed through with her threats. She never let you slide. In the long-run, Marcus knew that was good, it was the main reason he was able to go to a prestigious college like Stanford University. He just wished she would loosen the reins a little more often. She had this uncanny way to force you to comply with her expectations. It was pretty amazing how this skinny little nun of about five feet-nothing could command such respect from these hardened street urchins.

Marcus had a picture of his mother next to his bed. He had vague memories of her kindness to him and he remembered the love he felt for her. He was angered by her death, so he tried to bury it in the remotest part of his brain; he didn't want to think of it. He wished the police had found the gunman responsible for her death and that the perpetrator had been brought to justice. But Marcus knew the reality of the street and how callous it often is. Like many victims of crimes in the projects, Marcus' mom just didn't matter enough. She was a poor black, single mother; a statistic, a footnote that no one cared to read about, another casualty of poverty and neglect and indifference. If she was a blond-haired, blue-eyed, white girl living up on the Upper East Side, Marcus knew that her killer would have been found and would still be rotting away in prison. But she wasn't any of those things and that's just the way it is.

Marcus didn't even think of his father, the great disappointment. He didn't know who he was and never met him in his 18 years; and he never wanted to ever meet him, he thought. A man who fathers a child and takes no responsibility for his upbringing is a scoundrel. As far as Marcus was concerned his father was dead, not worth wasting his thoughts on. Marcus had a father; someone who cared for him, encouraged him, disciplined him, and loved him. Marcus thought he had all the father he needed in Sister Hannah.

The rest of the week went quickly for the boys, Friday was soon upon them. The Padres-Mets game in Queens was set for 7:00, but by 3:30 they were all ready to hop on the subway. They wanted to get there early to see batting practice. "Let's go," they implored Sister Hannah, "We have to catch the train out to Queens."

Sister Hannah assured them they would not miss batting practice. "Calm down boys. We won't be late. Our benefactor has arranged car service for us, to and from the park. We won't have to ride the trains tonight. I spoke to him earlier today. He wants us all to see number 800. He will be there tonight too and he is very excited about the possibility of Phil Perry hitting his 800th career home run. Maybe you guys will get to meet the man who pays all our expenses here on Greene Avenue."

About an hour later, two white stretch limousines drove up Greene Avenue and parked in front of the house. The boys stared at them. What was going on? Sister quickly said, "Hurry up guys. Our rides are here."

They looked at each other grinning wildly, shuffling their feet while they shadow–boxed and slapped each other's palms. None of them had ever been in a limousine, they were used to riding their bicycles or taking the subway to get places. This was extraordinary. "Hey Sister, this benefactor dude has a lot of money. Is he some rich white guy who feels sorry for us?"

Before she could answer Marcus spoke up, "So what if he is an old rich white guy? He helped us and he wasn't looking for anything from us. It's just like Sister says. It doesn't matter what you look like. Good people come in all shades and sizes. What is in the heart and in the soul is more important than what you look like. Ain't that the way it is, Sister?"

"That's right Marcus," she answered quietly.

The limousine ride to the Stadium, through Brooklyn and Queens, was both raucous and jovial as the boys wrestled, screamed and blasted music. They were rapturous in their glee and excitement. And oddly, Sister didn't tell them to tone any of it down. She let them enjoy their first ride in this monstrous car; she let them celebrate their youth, sitting peacefully in the front of the first car, chatting softly to the limousine driver.

When they got to the stadium, they lined up behind Sister Hannah. She handed the tickets to the usher and the usher counted the boys as they proceeded one by one through the turnstile. When the last boy was through, they huddled together and Sister instructed them to follow her and Marcus. They entered the lower loge and were escorted to front row seats behind the visitor's dugout. "Hey Sister, you didn't tell us how good these seats were. I thought we would be up in the nosebleed section. We're so close to the field, maybe we'll get to see Phil Perry."

"Perhaps," she answered coolly.

And when Perry came out for batting practice the boys were not disappointed. He smacked line drive after line drive, putting about a dozen balls into the outfield seats. After he finished, the boys called to him excitedly. And, then, the strangest thing happened. Perry walked slowly towards the Padres dugout, veered just to the right of the dugout and climbed into the stands. Sister stood up and walked down the row of seats towards Perry. She pointed at him and called his name, as if she knew him. He, in turn, walked towards her slowly and came upon her. He embraced her, giving her a gigantic bear hug, lifting her feet off the ground as he hugged her. Then he put her down. She slowly turned towards her boys and said, "Gentlemen, I'd like you to meet Phil Perry, one of my favorite former boarders."

The boys rushed towards them and looked on silently in awe. Phil shook each of their hands and spoke to each of them graciously. He came to Marcus last. He looked at him a little more intensely than he had at the other boys and said, "You must be Marcus. Sister has told me a lot about you. You're a good student and a football and track star, aren't you? I hear you will be out on the West Coast next year too. It is very nice to meet you."

"No disrespect, but how do you know all this about me, Mr. Perry?" Marcus asked quizzically.

"Sister writes me all the time. She keeps me updated on how things are working out on Greene Street. You know, I owe Sister everything; growing up, she was my mother and father all rolled into one. So I write her and she writes me, all the time. I wouldn't be here if it weren't for her. Hey Sister, how about I give you the ball I hit out tonight, number 800?"

'That sounds good Phil. Just don't be too smug; don't over-swing trying too hard for a home run. Number 800 will come when it's ready to come. Okay?"

"Gotcha. Well guys, I gotta go prepare for the game. Sister, can I invite you and the guys into the clubhouse after the game? We put out a nice spread for the players and their families. I would be honored if you joined me."

"We'll see," she answered, as Phil hopped back out of the stands and onto the field, descending into the dugout.

"Hey Sister," one of the boys called out, "when do we get to meet our mysterious benefactor?"

"You just did, Carlos. After all these years my secret is out. Phil Perry is the mystery man, the infamous anonymous benefactor."

"Cool," the boys all said almost in unison.

The boys settled in to watch the game. They had come to see a slugfest, to see Phil Perry hit his 800th home run. Instead, they saw a skillful pitchers' duel between the Padres ace Larry Wilson and the Mets ace Bennie Alvarez. Phil Perry and the rest of the Padres were completely mastered by the Mets Alvarez through the first eight innings this night. Perry struck out his first two at bats and looked to be pressing. Alvarez had his best stuff tonight and pitched almost flawlessly, getting 16 Padres in total to strikeout through the first eight innings. In fact, Alvarez was so dominant that the Padres were being no-hit through the first eight innings; and only three walks separated Alvarez from a perfect game. As the beginning of the ninth inning approached, the Mets held a 2-0 lead and a big picture of a smiling Alvarez flashed on the Diamond Vision screen with the following message, "No Met pitcher in the history of the franchise has ever pitched a no-hitter."

Excitement filled the ballpark. The top of the Padre order was scheduled up and the fans gave Alvarez a huge ovation as he strode to the mound. He was determined to make Met history. One time, long ago, Tom Seaver, Hall of Fame class of 1992, the greatest Met player of all-time, pitched a game at the old Shea Stadium and had a perfect game going into the ninth inning. He got the first two batters out, but the third batter hit a bloop single just out of reach of the second baseman; ruining perfection, before Tom Terrific retired the last batter. The rest of his life, Seaver always referred to that as the best game he ever pitched, his "almost perfect" game.

Alvarez made short, efficient order of the first two Padres in the inning, getting the leadoff hitter to pop up on the first pitch and striking out the second batter on four pitches. The crowd chanted "Bennie, Bennie", as Phil Perry strode to the plate. Alvarez had already struck out Perry his first two times at bat by blowing 98 mile per hour fastballs inside and high near Perry's fists. But now it was the ninth inning, and Alvarez was tiring, losing a little steam on his fastball. Would Alvarez challenge Perry, the greatest home run hitter ever, with fastballs or try to finesse him with off speed pitches?

The first pitch was a curveball on the inside part of the plate; strike one. Perry was annoyed; that was not a strike, he thought, the umpire is playing to the crowd of Mets fans. Perry guessed another off-speed pitch would come next and it did. He swung from his heels and connected the barrel of the bat with an inside curve ball. It was a towering blast towards the rightfield stands. Perry stood at home plate, still, gazing at the night sky. It would be either a home run or a long foul ball. Alvarez stood on the mound waving his arms, imploring the ball to go foul as it curved sharply towards foul territory.

In situations like this, sometimes the gods of physics favor the hitter and sometimes they favor the pitcher. Alvarez had pitched as well as he could, but tonight belonged to hitter, Mr. 800, Phil Perry; for although the ball continued to curve, it did not curve enough to give Alvarez his no-hitter. It hit the foul pole square on and bounded down into the stands. As the fans fought over the historic ball, Perry looked respectfully at Alvarez and tipped his batting helmet in his direction. The Diamond Vision screen lit up, saying simply "800!" Alvarez, initially angered at the loss of his no-hitter, gathered himself and shouted congratulations to Perry as he circled the bases. Slowly the stunned crowd of Met fans started to chant, "Per-ry, Per-ry, Per-ry." The chant grew so loud you could probably hear it all the way in New Jersey.

Perry emerged from the dugout and tipped his cap to the crowd. He looked up at Sister and the boys and said, "Sister Hannah, come down to the Clubhouse after the game."

When play resumed Alvarez struck out the final Padres hitter on three pitches. On this night he had struck out 18 batters, just one shy of Tom Seaver's Met club record. Like Seaver, Alvarez had pitched an almost perfect game. Met fans would have to wait another night for their no-hitter.

After the game, the boys from Greene Avenue were invited into the clubhouse by Phil Perry. The boys blended into the throng of people in the clubhouse, sampling generous portions of food off the buffet and chatting among themselves. A mob of reporters surrounded Perry and he talked about his career and about hitting home runs for about ten minutes before begging off, asking for a few minutes alone with his friend, Sister Hannah. He told Sister to bring along Marcus and they disappeared into a small room off the main locker room, filled with tables used to tape up the players.

"Sister, is this a good time? I don't know how to do this," Perry said awkwardly. He looked embarrassed and perplexed.

Sister interceded. "Marcus do you ever wonder about your Dad? Who he is? Where he is? Why you never saw him?"

"I'm not sure I want to know," said Marcus, "He might be in prison or he might be dead. You've done what you can to be both a father and a mother to me, Sister. I'm okay with that and with not knowing, I really am."

"Okay Marcus, but I'm going to let you in on a secret. Your father is right in front of you now. Phil is your Daddy. When he was a young kid, he lived with me in Brooklyn. He had nothing but his baseball talent. He didn't have your brains or your poise. He was shy and he was scared. When he went off to the Minor Leagues he vowed to try to someday have enough money to take care of you. When your Mom died, Phil asked that I take care of you. He didn't think he was mature enough."

"Marcus, Sister did such a wonderful job raising me, I thought it best if you got the benefit of her too. Once I hit the bigs, I had the money, but I thought Sister would do a better job than me in providing what you really needed. I wasn't sure I could handle the day-to-day responsibilities of being a single parent. Money is one thing, stability is another. I did what I thought was best for you."

Marcus stared at Phil for what seemed like a lifetime. He said nothing.

"Marcus, with all the money I've made, I can give you anything now."

"Everything but what I really wanted, Phil. You can't give me back those 18 years you weren't a part of my life."

"I'm sorry. I did all I thought I could. I didn't mean to… "

Marcus interrupted his father, saying, "Phil, there are three kinds of people in this world. Some look at a glass of water and say the cup is half empty, that's most people. They bitch and moan and complain.

But they aren't bad people, they're just ordinary people. That ain't me; I am not ordinary. Next, some people look at the cup of water and say its half-full, those people make the best of what the world gives them. Even when they feel betrayed or forgotten, those people spin it positively and make good of the situation. Then there is a third kind of person. The third kind of person looks at the cup and says who took my damn water? I'm going to kill that jerk, let me at him. Those people are angry and vengeful. They get even; even if it means getting mean. They want to get even with every person that ever short-changed them. And make no mistake Phil, for eighteen years, I do think you short-changed me. Before I knew who you were, I really looked up to you; local kid makes good. You used to be a hero, now you're just a man. I know which kind of person I am. So which kind of person do you think I am, Phil?"

Silence ensued for what seemed like forever. Phil despondently looked at Marcus' face, like a puppy that had just soiled his master's favorite chair. "Unfortunately, I'm not sure, Marcus. But I can tell you I thought I was doing what was best for you." said Phil sadly.

Sister smiled. "Go ahead, Marcus. Tell him; tell Phil what kind of man you are," she said.

"In this situation, as in most, I see this cup half-full. Yesterday, I had no father and now I have one. And he cared enough to check on me and support me and my adopted brothers financially. And he cared enough to give back to the lady that raised him. I am better off now than I was before today. Everything is cool. No hard feelings, man," Marcus said as he gave Phil a bear hug.

Sister Hannah beamed, saying "Good for you Marcus. I didn't do a bad job with Little Marcus, did I Phil?"

"No," answered Phil, "you did a great job. He's a better man than me."

Marcus broke free from the hug and smiled as he headed to the door. "Come on Dad, let's get something to eat," he said, "and if I'm going to be at Stanford, maybe you could sign next year with the Giants or the A's. That way we could hang out more often and you could see me run track. San Francisco and Oakland are a lot closer to Palo Alto than San Diego is. What do you think?"

"Not bad; you are a real thinker, Marcus. I like that. But don't say anything about that just yet, okay?"

"I won't say anything, on one condition. After I no longer live at Sister's house on Greene, you've got to promise to keep supporting her. Okay, benefactor?"

"Definitely, you have my word," said Phil.

"That's my boy," said Sister.

"No, that is OUR boy, Sister" said Phil proudly.

LaVergne, TN USA
05 October 2009
159919LV00001B/27/P